RIDDLE *of the*
RUBY RING

BAKER FAMILY ADVENTURES

RIDDLE *of the* RUBY RING

BY C. R. HEDGCOCK

"Where there is no vision, the people perish." —Proverbs 29:18

The Vision Forum, Inc.
4719 Blanco Rd., San Antonio, TX 78212
www.visionforum.com

ISBN   978-1-934554-95-1

Cover Design and Typography by Justin Turley

Printed in the United States of America

"God resists the proud,
but gives grace to the humble."

I Peter 5:5

TABLE *of* CONTENTS

A Word from the Author 13

Chapter 1 15

Chapter 2 25

Chapter 3 35

Chapter 4 43

Chapter 5 51

Chapter 6 61

Chapter 7 71

Chapter 8 81

Chapter 9 89

Chapter 10... 97

Chapter 11... 107

Chapter 12... 115

Chapter 13... 123

Chapter 14... 129

Chapter 15... 139

Chapter 16... 149

Chapter 17... 157

Chapter 18... 165

Chapter 19... 175

Chapter 20... 185

Chapter 21... 197

Chapter 22... 203

Chapter 23... 211

Chapter 24... 223

A WORD *from the* AUTHOR

"And whatever you do in word or deed, do all in the name of the Lord Jesus, giving thanks to God the Father through Him." —Col. 3:1

First of all, my acknowledgment is to my Lord and Savior Jesus Christ, in gratitude for His merciful provision of favor. Adventures really do begin when by grace we seek to obey Him!

To my dear parents, you have had an enormous impact in my life by your example and priorities. Thank you for seeking to instill in me the aspiration to use my talents for God's glory. As always, your input throughout the processes of story-writing has been invaluable.

To my siblings, Nicki, Christie, and Jonathan, your continued support, encouragement, and good advice has been a wonderful help. Rebekah, my oldest niece, your bright and cheery enthusiasm for the story was lovely!

To all my family and friends who have taken an interest in these writings, offered constructive criticisms, and given honest feedback—you have motivated me to set my sights higher and press forward to becoming a sharper tool for use in our Lord's service. In particular, thanks go to Joshua Lamprecht, Lorna Oliver, and "Uncle" Clive Hopkinson for their excellent suggestions.

Soli Deo Gloria!
C. R. Hedgcock

CHAPTER 1

The girl tightened her grip on the reins as her glossy black mount plunged through the woods. The horse lengthened his stride in obedience to her urging, but his nostrils flared and he began to pant hard with the exertion. Trees and logs whipped past, and forest creatures fled at the sound of the thundering hooves. The girl glanced backwards, fear in her hazel eyes. Her pursuer was gaining on her, and would be alongside in barely a minute.

She looked down at her tiring mount, and knew that fleeing would be fruitless. In a quick, brave motion, she turned her horse to face the enemy and clumsily drew a pistol from her belt. The other rider yanked his horse to a sudden stop, and the two faced each other tensely.

A grim smile slowly wrinkled the corners of the cowboy's eyes as he leaned back in the saddle. "Ooh, you've got a gun. I'm real scared now."

The girl pulled her lips into a tight line. "Don't move. I know you're out of powder, and I—I know how to use this."

"Sure ya do. Jus' like I know how to fly. Now gimme the gold."

The girl swallowed hard, and her chest heaved as a confused frown played on her face. "But—but I've got you covered. Don't move and I'll let you live."

The weathered cowboy yawned, tilting his Stetson back on his head. "That's enough foolin' around. Hand over the gold."

"I can't. It's not mine to give," the girl replied bravely, but her hands were trembling.

A moment passed in silence, and then with sudden, shocking dexterity, the cowboy flung himself to the ground and was alongside the black horse in a wink. He grabbed the pistol from the girl's hands, wrenching her from the saddle at the same time.

She shrieked in fright, kicking out and flailing her arms as the cowboy snatched the bag of coins from her pocket.

He gave a savage snarl. "Now get up. You're comin' with me."

The girl's eyes filled with terror, and she fainted as a sharp report rang out. The cowboy spun around with gritted teeth. The shot had not come from the gun he held.

A flash of brown, four-legged lightning streaked by. The horse causing this interruption skidded to a halt, and a young man leaped from the back of the dashing animal, one gun in either hand as he faced the cowboy.

"Leave Annie alone, coward!" he yelled.

"Shoulda known you'd be on my tail, Fred." The cowboy spat out the name in disgust.

The newcomer gazed at him steadily through clear, blue eyes. "Juan, hand over the stolen gold. I'm gonna escort you to—"

"Save yer breath!" the dark-haired, black-eyed Juan interrupted. "I'm not going nowhere with you!" He raised his pistol. "Duel."

Fred's sandy-colored eyebrows lowered beneath the line of his Stetson. "You know perfectly well that—"

The villain pulled the trigger, but nothing happened. In a frenzy, he leaped forward to attack, catching Fred off guard. As he did so, his boot caught on a hidden tree root and he stumbled to his knees. The gun flew out of his hands and landed a few feet away.

Fred looked surprised, but immediately regained control of the situation. His eyes were merry as he drawled, "Wa-al, that was easy."

Juan looked up with a grin. "Sorry."

"Cut!" came a loud call from the blonde, twelve year-old boy behind the camera. "Uh, I take it we'll have to try that scene again."

"Are you all right, Andy?" the girl asked, immediately "recovering" consciousness and pushing stray strands of wavy dark hair from her face.

"Yes, I'm fine," the cowboy responded as he raised himself to his feet and retrieved the model gun.

"That was a very well-acted scene," encouraged the camera-boy.

"And I got some great close-ups from here," a tall girl said from behind another camera.

Dark-haired Annie had just remounted when Fred pulled his watch out of his pocket.

"You know, I think we're going to have to forget about a re-take for now. Mother said lunch would be ready at two o'clock. We've got one quarter of an hour to get back."

"Can't we have a few more minutes?" Seth Wilbur, the camera-boy, asked.

Fred, or rather Phil Baker, shook his head. "We'd better not delay the lunch. Besides, just getting back to the stables and unsaddling the horses will take ten minutes."

They quickly gathered up the belongings and equipment they had taken down to the forest on the extremity of the Bakers' farm, and began walking in the direction of the house.

A young boy hurried up to the cowboy Juan. "Andy," he said, "could I please ride Sergeant back to the stables?"

"All right, Tom," Andy answered, hoisting the boy onto the back of his gray gelding.

"Hey Phil," Seth said, "why don't we record a short video introducing ourselves for the 'Behind the Scenes' feature? It won't take us any longer to get back."

"Good idea," Phil agreed. "Would you like to film it?"

"I sure would! Can I start with you?"

"You certainly may."

"All right!" Seth cried. "Three, two, one, action!"

"Hello everyone," Phil began, "and thank you for watching. I'm Phil Baker, the character of Fred and also the producer and co-director of this short film. Each of us has an acting role, and also contributes off-screen with things such as filming and costume designing. Allow me to introduce you to my younger brother Andy."

The boy looked blank for a moment as the camera was pointed at his face, but he quickly gave a confident smile.

"Hi!" He waved. "My name is Andrew Baker. I'm thirteen years old and I play the character of the bad cowboy, Juan. I'm also a cameraman and a co-director. Here, sitting on my horse, Sergeant, is my brother Thomas. How old are you, Tom?"

"I've just turned six," Tom replied proudly.

"What character do you play?"

Tom took a deep breath. "I pretend to be Annie's younger brother." He giggled. "It's kind of funny because that's what I am in real life!"

Seth chuckled as he moved the camera in the girls' direction.

"Hello," the girl on horseback said. "My name is Abby Baker and I'm Andy's twin sister. I'm the scriptwriter and one of the costume designers on this project, and I play the part of Annie. This is my horse Arrow, and he does a marvelous job of acting as Annie's horse, Coal Dust."

"Hi," the tall girl said, a little nervously, as Seth turned the camera to face her. "I'm Emily Wilbur. I'm fourteen and play the role of Annie's older sister, Sue. I've also helped Abby with the costumes and done a little of the filming."

Then Phil took the camera so that Seth could introduce himself. As he spoke, the others couldn't help grinning at his infectious enthusiasm and buoyancy.

"Hi there everybody, I'm Seth, Emily's handsome brother. I'm twelve years old, and I'm a cameraman on this project. It's my job to make sure that the character of Sheriff Beans remembers his lines. Oh, and I also do all my own stunts, which have included sitting, eating, and talking. It's pretty intense, but I manage somehow. Anyway, that's all for now, folks! Bye!"

Abby glanced at her brothers, Phil, Andy, and Tom, and thought back over how they had met their new friends, the Wilburs, and decided to make a short film with them. The Wilbur family had moved into the nearby farm a few months before, and had made immediate friends with the Bakers. There were five children in the Christian family, but only Emily and Seth, the two oldest, had gone out to the forest for the filming that day.

Emily, the oldest Wilbur child, came to walk beside Abby. The pretty girl was tall and athletic, with straight, honey-blonde hair and a side-swept bang that accentuated her green eyes. The two girls had quickly become good friends, and the more Abby got to know the older girl, the more she admired her.

Twelve-year-old Seth Wilbur was blonde with hazel eyes. He was stocky and quite short, but everybody was sure he would soon have a growth spurt. He and Andy had a lot in common, especially their sense of humor, love of cameras, and seemingly enormous appetites.

The children chattered all the way back to the stables, put the horses away, and then came quickly inside the house.

"Welcome back, film crew!" Mr. Wilbur greeted jovially. "Can I get autographs?"

The whole Wilbur family was there, having been invited by the Bakers for lunch, and there was much hustle and bustle to make the final preparations for such a large meal.

"Please wash hands, kids!" Mrs. Wilbur called from the kitchen, where she and Mrs. Baker were hurriedly dishing up lasagna before it got cold.

The children did as they were told, and then Abby slipped in to help carry out the plates while Andy poured juice. Finally, when they had all settled with steaming plates and mouthwatering aromas before them, Mr. Baker said grace. At first, talking was minimal as each person savored the first bites of rich lasagna, garlic bread, and a home-grown salad.

The Wilbur children had attended public school until a few years before, when their parents decided to start home-schooling instead. There were quite a few adjustments they had faced, and not all of them had been as easy to make as others. The biggest change, moving into the country, seemed much more appealing once the family met the Bakers.

Mr. Jedediah Wilbur was a strong man with a thick, dark brown mustache, and a warm, deep voice. He was an architect, and his tall, pretty wife Hannah had been a respected geneticist before starting to home-school their children.

"How's that film coming along?" Mrs. Wilbur asked the children.

"It's going well, thank you," Andy said.

"Phil, have you got any particular projects on at the moment?" Mr. Wilbur asked, interest showing on his friendly face.

"I'm studying the workings of electromagnetic waves," Phil said.

Mr. Wilbur's dark eyebrows rose. "Is that part of your course?"

"No." Phil shook his head. "It's got to do with something my father and I are working on."

Phil was still getting used to explaining that he was a fresh home-school graduate studying physics, mechanics, and engineering through an online correspondence course, and in his spare time helping his father. Mr. Baker was a self-employed engineer and inventor who labored tirelessly on new ideas in his large workshop.

"Very intriguing!" Mr. Wilbur said.

Mr. Baker nodded. "We're hoping to find practical applications for our discoveries. It's hard work, but worth it."

"How have you been doing with the new routine, Hannah?" Mrs. Baker asked.

"Quite well, thanks. We've got a load of boxes arriving from storage on Monday, and I know that's going to knock us out of schedule."

"Could we help you with those?" Mrs. Baker asked. "Many hands make light work."

Mrs. Wilbur's eyes widened. "Are you sure you can spare the time?"

"Of course! We'd be happy to."

"Well, that would be fantastic." Mrs. Wilbur beamed. "I'd really appreciate that."

****

Monday dawned two days later, sunny and clear, and the Baker children hurried to tackle their schoolwork and get all their chores done, which included looking after their horses and chickens, mucking out stables, and practicing their musical instruments. At three o'clock the twins, Tom, and their mother set off for the Wilbur farm.

The front door opened and Mrs. Wilbur's tall figure appeared. "Hello! Please come in."

The five Wilbur children rushed to greet everyone, welcoming the Bakers warmly. The younger boys, John and Zachary, immediately drew Tom's attention to a LEGO set they had just unpacked, and the two mothers headed straight for the kitchen. Abby, Emily, and seven-year-old Laura were the only ones left in the hallway.

Abby smiled at the two girls, unable to help admiring the way Emily looked. "How did you get your hair like that?" she asked.

"Oh, this?" Emily looked surprised. "Easy! Come on." She started to head upstairs. "Let's go to my room."

Abby and Laura followed up the stairs and down the corridor, and Abby glanced around the room in which she found herself. A loft bed was against one wall, with a desk under it, and boxes stood huddled up in a corner.

"Should we start unpacking?" Abby asked, motioning to them.

"Sure," Emily said, "that would be *awesome*. I'll get a pair of scissors to open the boxes." She shuffled the things on her desk, then moaned. "Ugh, *where* did Seth put them?" She stomped off to his room and returned a few moments later, waving them in the air. "See what I mean? He *never* puts things back!"

"Maybe he forgot," Abby suggested.

"Yes—every time!" She shook her head. "I'll talk to him later. Anyway, I'm the only one of us who doesn't have to share a room, which I'm really *relieved* about." She opened the nearest box. "Having to share personal space with siblings can be so annoying sometimes! Seth and John share because they always have, and Laura shares with Zac because he's scared by himself. You don't normally have to share a room, do you?"

"Not at home, but when we go on vacation, Tom and I do," Abby said.

"I—I don't mind sharing, actually."

Emily raised her eyebrows. "Oh?" She shrugged. "Well, you don't have the siblings I do!"

Abby didn't think that was the answer, but Emily quickly changed the subject.

"We have to start our schoolwork as soon as possible. We're already a week or so behind schedule, and you probably know just how hard it is to catch up on things."

Abby opened her mouth to state her agreement when Emily continued. "What are your favorite subjects?"

"History and English," Abby answered without hesitation. "Right now I'm learning about archeology, which is fascinating."

"Really? I've always thought it pretty dull. Oh, Abby?"

"Yes?"

"I'd really *love* to go for a ride around here with you when our horses arrive."

"I would too—I'm sure we can arrange something."

The girls talked and unpacked for an hour or so, and then came downstairs when it was time for a snack. One of the mothers had set out a large plate of peanut-butter cookies, which the boys were already hovering around.

"How have you girls got on with the unpacking?" Mrs. Baker asked.

"Very well, thanks," Emily said. "We've also had a great time chatting, haven't we, Abby?"

Abby felt an unexpected pressure at this question. *We?* she thought. *I haven't done much of the chatting. . . .*

"Sure," Abby said.

CHAPTER 2

The phone rang late on Wednesday afternoon, and Andy rushed to get it. "Good afternoon, Baker residence. This is Andrew speaking."

"Andy, this is Emily. Our horses have just arrived and we'd love for you and Abby to see them!"

"Thanks for letting us know. Just—"

"Oh, *please* ask Abby if she'd like to come on a ride with me."

"Now?"

"Yes!"

"Okay. Please hold on while I ask my parents if they mind." He was back at the phone in about ninety seconds. "We'll be there in ten minutes."

"Sounds *awesome*. Oh, Seth asks you to bring Sergeant."

"All right."

"Thanks. Bye!"

The twins finished doing the dishes, and then pulled on their jackets and riding boots. They raced down to the stables to tack up their two horses and then rode off to the Wilburs' farm.

All the Wilbur children were down at the stables, fussing over their horses and handing pieces of carrot and apple out generously.

"Andy, come see my ride," Seth called out, overly excited. He stood at the stable door over which the brown-and-white head of a paint horse looked out.

"He's called Geronimo," Seth said. "Gerry for short. Since he's a paint, I wanted to go with a Red Indian name—"

"Abby, come and meet Cappuccino," Emily said from inside the next stable. She was tacking up her big, palomino mare, and had perched the saddle on the stable door.

"Hello there," Abby said as the beautiful horse came forward to smell her hand. "The name fits her perfectly." She glanced at Emily's hair, pulled gently back into a braid, her bang neatly swooping the side of her forehead. Abby fingered her own wavy, chocolate-brown tresses which seemed suddenly boring by comparison.

Emily heaved the saddle off the door and onto the mare's broad back. "She's a lovely one to ride. You should feel how well she goes—I've never felt such a smooth canter from any other horse. We have to go easy on the horses today; my dad said nothing more than a little light exercise after their long trip."

John and Laura introduced the twins to the other two horses, and then Emily led Cappuccino around to the mounting block. Abby followed with Arrow, and Seth with Geronimo, while Andy slipped his boot into one stirrup, grabbed the saddle, and heaved himself up with ease.

"Neat." Seth nodded admiringly as he watched Andy. "I'm going to try that next time."

Andy just beamed.

They all checked the girths, and Seth tried to adjust his stirrups, insisting that he had grown since his last ride. Finally, when they were all ready, the boys and girls split up and rode separate ways.

"Seth!" Emily called over her shoulder. "We're not supposed to ride hard today—don't forget."

"I won't!" Seth grinned mischievously.

"Dad's orders, remember?"

"Yes, ma'am!"

Emily sighed as she turned back. "Brothers," she muttered.

"So, where were you thinking of riding?" Abby asked.

"Well, there used to be an old stable block in our north field, but we had it pulled down because it was really old and there's enough space for our horses in the new stables. There's a faint trail around there, which I thought we could head towards."

They chatted as they rode, not paying much attention to time or direction. Awhile later, they moved into a trot, enjoying themselves even more. Then, without warning, the horses spooked. Emily shrieked as Cappuccino bolted, nearly unseating her. Abby was thrown off balance as Arrow slammed to a stop mid-stride, his nostrils flaring. She clung tightly to his back, gasping in fright when she saw the object of the horses' terror.

Straight ahead gleamed the two eyes of a snake. It had raised its head, and was hissing loudly as its tail vibrated.

Abby's grip on Arrow's mane tightened and she leaned forward quickly as he reared. His hooves came down with a thud, sending the reptile slithering away through the grass. When it had disappeared beneath a mound of earth, Abby turned to see what had become of Emily. The girl seemed to be in control of Cappuccino again.

"Emily! Are you okay?" Abby called in a shaken voice, nudging the recovered Arrow into a walk.

"Not really." Emily swept her fringe aside and showed Abby her trembling hands. "That was really scary. I thought Cappuccino was going to dump me right on that snake!"

"I saw," Abby said, nodding. "Well done for staying on. It was a dangerous situation, and I thank the Lord we got out of it safe and sound."

"Well. . . ." Emily hesitated. "Safe, maybe, but not so sound. I'm not going to be able to ride again until I know that horrible creature is gone. Was it a rattlesnake?"

"It looked awfully like one."

Emily gasped, her hand on her heart. "To think we were attacked by a rattler! Oh my goodness! How dangerous! I could have died!"

"I was just going to suggest we find the boys and ask them to kill it."

"What? The boys?"

"Andy should be able to, but I suppose it might be wiser to ask Phil to kill it instead."

"Yes, I think so too—wait, do they have to kill it?" Emily looked more shocked than before.

"Look, if it's a rattler, then it's a dangerous creature. Just imagine it had managed to bite Cappuccino—or you, or Laura, or Zac, for that matter. There would be serious consequences. Anyway, you can ask your dad what to do."

"Oh, he's not at home right now. He had to do something for business."

"You ask your mother then, while I tell the boys what happened."

"Okay. Here's my phone. Call Seth and tell him to meet you at the stables." Emily urged Cappuccino into a trot. "I think I'll go home and get something to calm me down."

Abby arranged to meet the boys at the stables, where she told them what happened. They were both eager to set out immediately, and had already gathered up what they thought they'd need when Seth's phone rang.

"Hello? Yeah." Seth frowned. "We'll be fine on our own; Andy knows just what to do. But—okay. Okay, we'll do that. Bye." He pulled the phone away from his ear. "That was Emily. She spoke to our mom, who thinks we should ask someone to help us, either your dad or Phil."

"It's a good idea," Abby said.

"I don't need help," Andy disagreed with unusual force. "Last time there was a snake on our farm, Father practically let me take care of it myself."

"That wasn't a rattlesnake," Abby countered.

"I'm not scared."

Abby frowned at Andy's strange behavior. For the last few days he had seemed to be acting with quite a bit of bravado. "I'm sure you're not afraid, but obviously Mrs. Wilbur thinks supervision is a wise precaution."

Phil walked down to the stables a few minutes later, having driven over to the farm. He had a backpack on, out of which protruded a long forked stick.

"I heard there was very nearly a serious accident involving a rattlesnake," he announced.

"Yes, and we've already gathered up all the things we'll need to catch it," Seth said. "Andy's got the spade, and I've got the First Aid kit and a phone. Abby thinks the snake slid into a hole, and I'm not really sure how we'll get it to come out."

Phil nodded. "I've brought matches, in case we need to smoke the creature out, as well as a few other supplies. The easiest way to get it out would be to flush its hole with water, but for that we'd need a faucet and hose."

"Oh, we've got a short hose-pipe in the store room," Seth said.

"That won't be much use without a faucet," Phil said.

"Well," Seth said, "you girls were near the old stables when the horses got a fright, weren't you?"

Abby nodded.

"I spotted a faucet a few evenings ago when I watched the crew demolish it."

"Good!" Phil said. "We can only hope the hose is long enough."

"Yep. I'll go get it," Seth volunteered.

"Where's Emily?" Abby asked Phil.

"I stopped over at the house before coming down here, and she said she needed to recover from her fright and wouldn't be joining us. How big was the snake?"

"About three feet long, and quite thick."

"What color?"

"It was cream, with dark brown blotches all over its back."

Seth returned bearing a coiled hose-pipe, which he offered to carry for Phil, slinging it over one shoulder and under the other arm. Phil borrowed one of the Wilburs' horses, and then they set off the way the girls had traveled earlier that day.

When they finally got to the spot the girls had first seen the snake, Abby

29

pointed to the grass and described the series of events. "The snake slithered that way and disappeared behind that mound."

Phil urged his mount onwards at a cautious walk, then paused. "The snake disappeared here?"

"That's right."

"Well," Seth said, "this isn't *near* the foundations of the old stables—this *is* the foundations of the old stables!"

Phil dismounted, and the others hurried to do the same. They all carefully approached the foundations.

"There!" Abby whispered. "Look at that hole! That must lead to the snake's den."

Phil spotted the faucet nearby and connected the hose to it. Then he opened his backpack and set out a large, clear plastic container with holes in the lid and grasped the long handle of the forked stick he'd brought.

"You all stay back and behind me," he instructed. "If this is a rattlesnake, which the evidence certainly points to, we don't want to take any chances."

"Phil, last time Father let me do it," Andy said.

"He didn't give you permission this time," Phil answered, the moment's tension obviously affecting him, "but you certainly can help if suitable. Now that I think of it, you can be in charge of the faucet. Everybody, keep your eyes open. This hole could have more than one entrance."

He positioned himself above the mound. With one hand he hovered the forked stick over the mouth of the hole, and with the other he pointed the hose down it. He nodded, giving Andy the signal to turn the faucet. A moment later, water spluttered from the hose and streamed into the hole.

The tension built as the children looked around, at any moment expecting to see the snake appear from any crevice or behind any mound. Seconds passed. They stared at Phil. Nothing seemed to be happening. More time ticked by.

Seth licked his dry lips and glanced at Andy, whose hand still rested on the faucet.

"Maybe it's the wrong hole," he said, when a long figure suddenly appeared. Acting quickly, Phil brought the forked stick down behind the creature's head, pinning it to the ground.

"Got it!" the others cried as Phil breathed again.

Andy turned off the water as Phil paused to examine the creature. It was very agitated, hissing loudly from time to time, flattening its head, and vibrating its tail. The others came to get a closer look, and Seth snapped a photo.

"This is some kind of pine snake," Phil eventually said.

"You mean it's not a rattler?" Seth asked.

"That's right," Andy said quickly, trying to get a word in.

"See, it has a rather slender head and no rattle on its tail. Pine snakes aren't venomous, and are known to be rattlesnake look-alikes," Phil said.

Seth did not look convinced. "But how can you be completely sure it's not a rattler that's lost its rattle?"

Phil smiled quickly. "Rattlers are pit vipers. Take a look at this one's eyes. The pupil is round—"

"Whereas pit vipers have elliptical pupils, like cats," Andy interrupted.

"Yes. Further, pit vipers have a deep pit on each side of the head, roughly between the eye and nostril. This one doesn't. For these reasons, it can't be a pit viper, and therefore it can't be a rattlesnake."

"See? Easy to tell the difference," Andy said in conclusion.

None of them noticed Abby's disturbed frown. *What has gotten into Andy?* she wondered.

"Here's the spade." Seth offered the tool to Phil.

"No thanks, Seth. Since it's not venomous, I won't kill it."

"Emily will be relieved," Abby muttered.

"But we don't want snakes on our property!" Seth's eyes widened. "You're not going to let it go, are you?"

"I won't if your family would prefer that," Phil said, "but they're great for catching rats. These snakes are also sometimes kept as pets, so . . . do you want it?"

Seth shook his head quickly. "No thanks!"

"And you're sure your parents don't want a resident rat-catcher?"

"If we did, we'd get a cat," Seth said decisively.

"In that case, we'll have to take it away from here to set it free. Andy, could you get the burlap bag, please?"

Phil crouched and grasped the snake behind its head, picking it up as he did so. He dropped it into the bag Andy held up and quickly closed the bag.

"Whew!" Seth breathed, wiping his brow. "That was exhausting."

"I know just what you mean," Abby agreed, "and we didn't even do anything!"

"We're not done yet," Phil said. "We have to take this fellow away. Hopefully it just burrowed itself a nice hole to live in, but there's a chance it laid eggs down there."

"Eggs?" Seth exclaimed. "Oh no!"

"And an interesting thing about pine snakes," Andy said, "is that they lay huge eggs. If I remember correctly, the hatchlings are over one foot long!"

Phil nodded. "Sometimes up to seventeen inches, actually. From what Father said, these snakes can range from about four to eight feet long in adulthood. This one must be pretty young."

Phil put the burlap bag inside the container with air-holes, put that inside his backpack, and then remounted. They all rode back to the stables and piled into the Bakers' car. Phil drove a few miles down a country road, and then stopped at a patch of open land to set the snake free.

CHAPTER 3

Upon returning to the Wilbur farm, the boys and Abby spoke to Mrs. Wilbur about the incident.

"Are you troubled by the idea of a couple of non-venomous snakes on your property?" Phil asked.

Mrs. Wilbur nodded. "The idea is unsettling, especially when thinking about our younger children. They wouldn't be able to tell the difference between a pine and a rattler, which is dangerous."

"That's a good point," Phil said. "Clearly the eggs haven't hatched yet, if there are any, else the hatchlings would've come out when I flushed the burrow with water. I thought I'd head back down there to dig carefully away at the hole and see what's in there."

"Thank you," Mrs. Wilbur said. "We have plenty of spades and shovels. Maybe you should drive down to save yourselves carrying them all the way."

They followed up on that advice, loading the digging implements into the Bakers' trunk before driving through the fields in the fading evening light. Emily and John had decided to join them.

"This is the hole our snake friend was in." Phil peered at the hole. "There's a chance that a pet shop might be interested in some eggs. We should dig carefully."

Phil and Andy set to work, carefully enlarging the hole, while the girls and John cautiously examined the rest of the foundations. The girls were peering at a shallow hole when there was a sudden hiss and something jolted their backs. Emily squealed and Abby's heart pounded as she swung around. Seth chuckled mischievously as he bounded away.

"Got ya! Hissssssss!" he repeated.

"Come on, Seth!" Emily retorted, angry at being given a fright. "We're trying to concentrate here. Do something useful for a change!"

His expression turned sulky, but he soon became absorbed in watching the other boys digging. Abby felt sorry about the way Emily had spoken to him. *I know we're not supposed to vent our feelings but . . . but this particular case is not really any of my business*, she tried to persuade herself.

John began stomping around the foundations, stopping every now and then to stoop low and poke around in the dirt. Then he started jumping up and down.

"What *are* you doing?" Emily finally asked.

"Listen," he said, jumping again.

"What do you hear?" Abby asked.

"I hear nothing," he said.

The girls exchanged confused looks.

"Nothing," he repeated. "I hear a hollow space, like there's nothing below this."

He jumped again, and the girls could hear an empty thud as he landed.

Andy, who had paused from his digging, went to investigate. He knelt, put his ear close to the ground, and rapped his knuckles on the earth. Seth was watching with interest.

"It's hollow!" Andy cried as he tapped the ground beside John's shoes. "The rest seems solid, but this little patch here sounds hollow!"

"How did you discover this, John?" Abby asked.

"I first heard it when Seth ran away from you girls," he said in his quiet way. "One or two of his steps sounded different, and I wanted to know why."

Andy grabbed a small hand-shovel and began digging away at the hard earth. Then it jammed and wouldn't go any further.

"That's wood—I'm sure of it!" he exclaimed. "Hey, Phil! Come and have a look here!"

"What is it, And?"

"Something hollow under here," Andy said.

"I'm busy with this," Phil said, "but let me know what you find."

"Quick, Seth, get a spade," Andy said, scraping furiously with his hand-shovel. The other boy complied, and they both set to work until sweat glistened on their foreheads.

"There's definitely something solid under this layer of earth." Andy huffed as his shovel struck a hard object. In a few minutes they had exposed a small area of wood.

Seth rapped his knuckles against it and everybody could hear the resonant sound that resulted.

"Let's pull up the wood and see what's under it!" Seth exclaimed.

The boys continued, uncovering several small planks. The girls watched.

"Isn't it strange," Emily said, "that this wood isn't rotten? I mean, it must have been here for years."

"Maybe the stables kept rainwater off it," Abby said.

"Yes," Andy agreed. "This wood is old, but seems pretty sturdy. I don't know how we're going to get it all up."

"Will we have to saw it?" Seth asked.

"I don't think so," Abby said. "Look."

They all leaned over to see the dull metal objects she was pointing at.

"Hinges!" Andy said. "A trapdoor! Let's see if it will still open."

They went around to the opposite side to finish digging out the other end of the wood while John fetched another shovel. Then the two boys grabbed the edge of the trapdoor and tried to lift, but it wouldn't budge.

By this time, Phil had stopped digging and come closer to watch.

"We need a wedge of some sort," Andy said. He grabbed a spade and slipped it under the wood as a lever. John offered his services, helping to pry around the lid of the trapdoor. The three of them tried again and again to lift it, until there was a long squeal from the hinges and the door suddenly came loose.

The girls held their breath as the boys strained under the heavy trapdoor and the stubbornness of the hinges. Phil dived in to help, while the girls each grabbed one side of the door, and with the combined effort they all managed to lift it up to a vertical position and then lower it down the other side.

"Whew," Andy sighed, straightening up. "Those hinges . . ." he trailed off as he peered into the space below. "Phil!" he called. "I think you would want to see this!"

"I'm right here," Phil said, rubbing the ear that had just endured a blast of volume.

"Oh—oops." He grinned. "Sorry."

"We found a secret hide-out!" Seth whooped excitedly. "Just look at it!"

Phil straightened up to stare at the hollow.

"This is amazing," he said.

From what Phil could see, it was lined with stone, and a few wooden crates were all that could fit into the small space.

"Can we open the crates?" Seth asked.

"I don't know." Phil's voice was tinged with amazement. "We can only guess how old these are, and don't want to damage them."

Abby almost laughed. "This is like pretending to be an archeologist—except it's really happening!"

Andy helped Phil haul one heavy crate out of the hollow, and then they both proceeded to pry it open, very carefully, using their pocket-knives. The lid came off in a few minutes, and everybody watched as Phil shifted away the wood shavings and gently pulled out an old glass bottle.

"Is that all?" Emily asked in disbelief.

"There's more of them in here," Phil said, moving the wood shavings to reveal a crate full of the bottles.

Emily shook her head. "I mean, is that all that was hidden here? Glass bottles?"

"It seems so," Phil said. "I have a feeling that when this was built, it wasn't intended to be a secret hollow at all. Rather, this may have been used many years ago as a miniature cellar. Then, as years passed, it became a convenient place to hide things."

"What's in the bottles?" John asked, peering at the liquid inside.

"I can't be sure, but my guess is alcohol," Phil said. "It was illegal in the United States in 1919, and that may be why it was hidden. I think we had better head inside to see properly. It's getting dark and we don't want to damage anything."

"What about that snake hole?" John asked.

"Oh, I'd forgotten about it," Phil admitted. "I can probably come over and continue working on it tomorrow, if necessary. For now, I think everybody is itching to find out more about these crates. It's a good thing we brought the car along and don't have to lug them all the way to the house."

They all helped to haul the remaining crates from the hollow and load them into the trunk, Andy insisting that he didn't need any help. Andy had his flashlight with him, which proved to be of great assistance in the gathering darkness. Before leaving the site, Phil and he carefully verified that nothing was left in the cellar and replaced the trapdoor.

When they arrived at the house, Mrs. Wilbur was greatly intrigued to see her children weighed down with old crates.

"Where exactly did you find these?" she asked.

"In the cellar," Seth said casually, stifling a grin.

"What cellar?" she asked in surprise.

"The cellar under the old stables."

By the time the children explained the whole story, all the crates were lined up in the garage, with the first one ready for inspection. Phil removed the identical glass bottles, looking closely at each one. The others then watched him open the other crates. Each crate contained the same number of glass bottles, surrounded by wood shavings.

"How did the wood shavings survive if they're really so old?" Emily asked with a frown.

"The cellar was lined with stone and had a sturdy trapdoor over it, and all that was beneath the shelter of the old stables," Phil explained. "In the absence of moisture, heat, air, and light, the crates—and their contents—would be well preserved."

"Just like the Egyptian mummies, I suppose," John said.

"Yes, something like that." Phil dug his hand in the wood shavings to make sure the third crate was empty. He frowned, paused, and then pulled his hand out of the crate more quickly than usual.

"What's wrong?" Abby asked.

"I guess I was startled to feel something smooth in there," Phil said.

"Smooth?" The boys' eyes widened.

Phil said no more, but busied himself in shifting the wood shavings away from one corner of the crate. The others crowded around even closer, eager to see what he had discovered. He gave a grunt of surprise and pulled out a small leather pouch.

Most of the others were too curious to say anything, and watched in tense silence as Phil opened the pouch and peered steadily inside. Seth was one exception.

"What's inside? What is it?" he asked.

Phil shook his head and gave a low whistle. "Somebody get me a paper towel, please."

Abby tore a piece off the roll and laid it on his hand. Then, delicately, he tipped the leather pouch over and a small, circular object tumbled out.

The others gasped. On the paper towel in his hand lay a yellow band of metal with a dark red jewel set into one side. Delicate metalwork surrounded the jewel, enhancing its beauty.

"A ring!" Mrs. Wilbur exclaimed, leaning forward to study it.

"Do you think it's gold?" Abby asked.

"I'm not sure," Phil said. "The detail is amazing. Would you like a closer look?"

Everybody eagerly took a turn to inspect the ring, and in the meantime, Phil checked the other crates for hidden surprises like the leather pouch, but found none.

"Will we be able to keep the ring?" Emily asked. "Please?"

"I don't know," Mrs. Wilbur said. "We should find out who it belongs to. Even though it might be worth quite a lot, it might also have personal value to somebody."

Mrs. Wilbur left to fetch a soft cloth with which to polish the ring and Seth quickly filled in the silence.

"See, Emily?" Seth said. "If it wasn't for my little joke, John wouldn't have heard the hollow sound, and we wouldn't have found any of this. I'm not so useless after all."

Emily gave him an uncomfortable look, trying to avoid the fact that the discovery really was owed, in some small way, to him.

"I never said you were useless," Emily hedged.

Mrs. Wilbur returned gently rubbing the ring with a soft cloth.

Abby sighed as she watched. "What a pretty ring. I only wish I knew its story."

CHAPTER 4

The next day was a busy one for both families, and only late in the afternoon did the twins invite Emily and Seth to come over and see their chores routine.

"Come on in," Abby welcomed when the siblings arrived at the Bakers' door. She led them into the living room while Andy brought his schedule down from upstairs.

"So you feed your horses before breakfast?" Seth asked, a little surprised, as he looked at the page.

"Don't be shocked." Andy grinned. "Young people get things done quickly when they're hungry."

"Ha ha," Seth replied dryly, not very excited by the idea.

After a few more minutes of discussing the routine, Emily brought up the subject the twins had been wondering about all day.

"My dad examined the ring carefully today," she said with a confidential air.

"And?" the twins chorused, leaning forward.

Seth cleared his throat. "Dad says the—"

"Start with the bottles," Emily interrupted.

"You start with the bottles—I want to tell about the ring."

"But I was the one to start the conversation! I want to tell about the ring!"

Seth frowned. "You always want to tell the more important part of a story."

"So do you!"

Abby and Andy exchanged uncomfortable glances.

"Hello," a voice interrupted. It was Phil, who had just come downstairs. There was silence as both Emily and Seth suddenly felt very immature indeed.

"Hi Phil," Seth said, color rushing into his cheeks.

"Hi," Emily said sheepishly.

Phil responded pleasantly. "Are you both well?"

"Uh, yes, thanks," Seth said.

Emily nodded.

"Glad to hear that," Phil said. "Anyway, please excuse me; I'm on my way to the workshop." With that, he left the room.

An awkward silence followed, in which Emily squeaked, "You can tell about the ring."

"No, that's okay. You can," Seth said.

"I don't want to."

"Well, as we were saying," Seth resumed, trying to forget what had just happened, "my dad examined the crates and judged them to be about one hundred years old. As for the ring, my dad says it's gold and is made in the design of the 1600s!"

"The 1600s!" Abby gasped. "That sounds very valuable."

Emily nodded. "Our dad has already contacted the local newspaper. He's going to write an article about the ring for the Monday paper. If we can find the true owner, we might discover who made it and where it came from."

"How fascinating," Abby said. "I hope we get to hear the story behind it."

"What kind of story can a ring have, anyway?" Andy asked. "A very dull one, I'd guess. 'Dear Diary, Lady Abby wore me today until she had to wash the laundry in the river. Then she put me in her pocket. Then she put me on again. Then she took me off again . . .'"

"Come on, Andy!" Abby protested, giving her twin a playful shove. "Have a little imagination—for all we know it could have belonged to the Queen of Sheba."

"And now it needs to be restored to her family," Andy teased.

"Exactly."

Seth roared with laughter. "You guys are *hysterical*!"

"Abby," Andy spluttered, "I think you have a little too much imagination—"

"And you have none, so we make a good pair!" Abby laughed, at that moment noticing just how distant Emily and Seth were as siblings, reflected in their posture and their distance from each other.

"Anyway," Emily said once the laughter subsided, "my parents said that if nobody claims the ring, maybe I can have it."

"That would be lovely," Abby said.

"And," Emily added, "our dad found an inscription on the inside of the ring. He still doesn't know what it means, but he'll try figure it out."

A little later, Mr. Wilbur arrived to fetch Emily and Seth. "I was on my way home, and knew they were here, so I thought I may as well pick them up," he told Mrs. Baker cheerfully.

Mrs. Baker nodded. "Can I get you some coffee?"

"No, but thank you for offering. I'll be on my way soon."

"Have you got any news about the ring yet?" Emily asked eagerly.

"Yes," Mr. Wilbur said. He turned to the Bakers. "Did my kids tell you about the inscription on the inside?"

"Yes," the twins said in unison.

"It was in Latin, and, my Latin being a little rusty, it took me awhile to figure out what the inscription said."

"Do you know it now?" Seth sounded ready to burst.

"Yes, I do. The inscription was '*supter in medius*,' which translates into 'beneath the middle.' A strange clue, if you ask me, or maybe just a fake clue as somebody's idea of a practical joke."

"I wonder if practical jokes existed back then," Seth said.

His father chuckled. "The ring may have been inscribed more recently than the 1600s. In fact, it could have been made recently and just in the style of the seventeenth century."

"Do you have any idea what the significance of the inscription could be?" Abby asked.

Mr. Wilbur shook his head. "None at all."

"It must mean something very important." Abby wrung her hands. "Oh, how intriguing! Would you mind if we do some research about it?"

Mr. Wilbur laughed. "I'm sure it's not as exciting as you seem to think, but I don't mind at all."

"Why, thank you!" Abby's eyes shone. "Mother, would it be a problem?"

"I don't see why it would be."

Sure enough, as soon as the Wilburs left, Abby sat down at the laptop she and Andy shared and typed "1600s rings" into the search engine. She scrolled down the list of results, frowned, and then modified her search to "1600s ruby ring." Articles with pictures of rings matching that description came up, but none were the same as the ring they had found.

Her enthusiasm somewhat dampened, she tried to look up "1600s jewelers." She was reading a long article when Phil came and peered over her shoulder.

"What are you up to?"

She quickly explained the situation, then sighed. "I can't seem to find any related information. To be honest, I'm not sure what I'm looking for."

Phil nodded in thought and pulled a seat next to his sister's. "What we really need to find out is who lived on the Wilburs' farm when those crates were hidden away. It would make sense that whoever hid the ring, owned it."

"Great idea! Unless—" Abby paused. "Unless the ring was hidden because it had been stolen."

"Whatever the case, we can still assume it was hidden at the same time as the crates."

"So—how are we going to find out who lived there?"

Again Phil looked thoughtful. "We might be able to ask someone who has lived in the area long enough."

"Mr. Wilbur says the crates are one hundred years old," Abby said as Andy joined them.

"I don't *think* we know anyone that age," Andy said with a grin.

"Well, not exactly," Phil admitted. "My idea isn't completely unhelpful, though. Mr. Davis from church is about eighty-five years old, I'd guess, and he just might know who lived on the Wilburs' farm before he was born. We could call him."

Mrs. Baker thought Phil's idea was a good one, and a few minutes later he was dialing the number of the kindly old gentleman. After exchanging greetings, Phil plunged into the story.

"We don't know who the crates and the ring belonged to, and that's why we want to find out who lived on the Wilburs' farm around 1919," he finished.

The phone was on loudspeaker so the others could hear too. Mr. Davis's voice was slow and methodical as he replied.

"I was born in 1927, so I wasn't around at the time, but to the best of my knowledge that farm belonged to the Larone family for many generations. They moved out when I was about ten, because Mr. Larone had lost his job and was deeply in debt. That was just before Mrs. Larone had their baby son. He's grown up now, and his nickname is Bud. I think he lives out towards Bridgeton."

Phil was alert. "So we're looking for a man named Mr. Bud Larone?"

"Yes. He might have some family records that could prove that his parents lived on the farm in 1919."

"That sounds promising," Phil said.

Mr. Davis hummed in agreement. "If my memory serves me correctly, he used to have an interest in archeology."

"Archeology?" Abby repeated in surprise. "I've just been learning about that."

"Do you have Mr. Larone's phone number?" Phil asked.

Mr. Davis thought for a minute. "I'm not sure; we haven't been in contact for a very long time. I'll look and let you know if I have it." He hesitated. "I've just got to warn you to be cautious. He may be different now, but he used to be quite a crafty sort, managing to make things go in his favor. He might try to get something from you if he can."

CHAPTER 5

A meeting with Bud Larone was arranged for the next afternoon, and the Bakers prayed that Phil would know how to handle the "situation," as Mr. Davis had described it. At three o'clock, Phil, Andy, and Seth found themselves on the porch of a large old house. The front garden consisted of a healthy green lawn bordered by beds of brightly colored flowers.

"What? You're just kids?" the seventy-something-year-old man asked as he opened his front door.

"Hello, Mr. Larone," Phil said pleasantly, trying to ignore the man's cold words. "I am Philip, this is my brother Andy, and our friend Seth."

"Humph. Pleased to meet you, I suppose. Well, you'd all better come inside."

That hasty introduction being the only one they were likely to get, they followed old Mr. Larone inside his house. They were surprised by his tactless remarks, and hoped he would become more friendly as the visit progressed.

He led the boys into the living room, where he motioned for them to sit down.

"So, you said on the phone that you wanted to talk about a farm nearby that your friends moved into."

Phil exchanged a quick glance with Andy and then cleared his throat. "Yes, Mr. Larone. Our friends have moved into what was formerly called Lucky

Horseshoe Ranch and Mr. Davis said that it belonged to your family for a long time."

"That's right," Mr. Larone grunted, settling his withered frame into an armchair that matched the shabby tinge of the rest of the house.

"Could I ask what year your family left?"

"It was the year I was born, 1937."

"Do you know when your family first moved in?"

Mr. Larone frowned, deepening the creases on his drawn face. "Why on earth would you want to know that?"

"Uh—" Phil paused. "Was your family there around 1919?"

"Of course! Larones have lived there for generations! Why are you interested?"

"Well, we found a small cellar on the property. In it were old crates, which we think are from around the year 1919, and we want to find who owned them. Since your parents lived on the farm in that year, we wondered if they told you about storing them."

Mr. Larone's icy expression slowly melted and a surprised one took its place. His bony knuckles turned white as he gripped the armrests of his chair.

"Crates?" he said, his throat dry. He licked his lips and tried again. "Crates with bottles in them?"

Andy and Seth exchanged secretive glances.

"That's right," Phil answered.

"Bottles, and nothing else?"

Phil considered his words carefully. "Should there be anything else in them?"

"No, no, no, of course not," Mr. Larone said quickly. Then, eying Phil for a moment, he slowly stammered, "Well, you might have found jewelry. Maybe . . . a ring."

The boys' faces must have shown their surprise because Mr. Larone scoffed, "Ha! So it was a test! You weren't going to tell me about the ring because you wanted to see whether I knew about it or not."

"Could you describe the ring?" Andy suggested.

"Another test, eh?" Mr. Larone said in contempt, wrinkling the corners of his eyes. "I can describe it, and more than that, I can tell the story of it. My ancestor was a man named Haggai Larone, but this story is mainly about his youngest brother, Hank, when he was a young fellow living in the tiny town of Patience. At the time, it was one of the most westerly places white men had dared to settle, and it was rare for visitors of any sort to pass by."

Mr. Larone sat comfortably back as he settled into his story. He rested his hands on his legs, but they kept on jumping up whenever he felt that illustration was necessary. Phil had the idea to record the story on his phone so his family members could hear it too.

"Now, young Hank had grown up in very difficult circumstances, being the youngest of five children, with a dead mother and a drunkard father. Nobody expected much to come of him or his siblings, except that they would become lazy drunkards too when they grew up. Fearing this, one of the men in town took a personal interest in their welfare and tried to train good habits in them, as much as was possible for him to do. Now when Hank was only about fourteen years old, his father got in trouble for stealing. He fled the town, taking his children with him—but did he take Hank? No, no. Nobody wanted Hank. His own father fled the town and left him behind."

Mr. Larone paused here for awhile to make his point. When he felt he had done this, he continued.

"The townsfolk felt sorry for the boy, so they decided to each pay a little towards his upkeep and education. The beloved town doctor, Dr. Clark, had a spare room in his house and agreed to let Hank live there, provided that he make himself useful. After two years, Dr. Clark could see that Hank was a smart kid, and thought he had the potential to become a doctor one day.

"Hank began studying medicine and learning as much from Dr. Clark as he could. He would help Dr. Clark treat bullet wounds, perform amputations, help sick animals, and prescribe medicine for diseases. In time, he became almost as knowledgeable as the doctor himself—but he'd never got the chance to prove this.

"One night, the rain set in with a vengeance and the townsfolk feared flooding. Hank was staring out his window when he saw the dark shape of a wagon roll slowly down the road. He called out to Dr. Clark, and together they went out to see if they could help the man driving the wagon. He was wrapped up tightly in his drenched coat, doubled over, and apparently asleep. His horse was exhausted and soaking wet, its legs covered in mud.

"Hank and Dr. Clark worked quickly. They managed to pull the man off the wagon and carry him into the house, and then Hank rushed out again to bring the horse and wagon into the dry stable. When he came back to the house a moment later, Dr. Clark said, 'You discovered this man who needs our help. That's why I'm going to make him your first assignment. What do we need to do for him?'

"'First, we need to get him out of his wet clothes and make him as warm and dry as possible,' Hank replied.

"They worked together with the stiff and cold man, and in a few minutes had him wrapped in warm blankets in the patient's room, with a few logs alight in the fireplace. Hank heated up some soup, in case the man should awake, and watched him while Dr. Clark went out to properly look after the exhausted horse.

"The rain eventually let up, but the man didn't awake all night. He stirred a little the next morning, coughing terribly, and drank a bit of the soup Hank offered him before falling asleep again. Dr. Clark and Hank took turns to rest and to watch the patient, giving him warm soup and a blend of medicinal herbs every time he woke up—I don't know, a bit of elderberry, ginger, or ginseng, I guess. Towards the end of the day, color returned to his face and he was well enough to sit up in bed and feed himself a little, though he had several coughing fits.

"By the next evening, the man assured the doctors that he was well enough to be on his way and look after himself. He didn't have any money with him, but paid Hank with a gold, ruby-set ring in return for saving his life. Then he hitched his recovered horse to the wagon and made his way to the town pastor's house, where he spent the night.

"The next morning he began selling his goods straight from his wagon, setting up a sign which read, 'Victor James' Goods.' The townsfolk came to see the stuff, mainly out of curiosity. He had things which he traded from the Indians, you see, so they bought his stock pretty eagerly.

"Hank came to the church the following morning, along with the rest of the townsfolk, and the pastor announced that the trader would be saying a few words before the sermon. Victor stood up and went to the pulpit, where he introduced himself as a trader and missionary to the Indians. He began to talk about something—I don't know what it was, only that Hank didn't take long to decide that there was something sinister about this fellow.

"After church there was a feast at the pastor's house, which all the members were invited to attend. Well, at this feast, Hank only got more uneasy as the stranger managed to win more and more people over to liking him.

"The next day, Hank went to Victor's wagon to have a look at his goods. He still had the suspicious feeling about the man, which he couldn't quite place. Still, Hank was surprised when Victor asked for the ring back. Hank had already promised it to the girl he was going to marry, so he refused. Victor got angry and made threats, but Hank stood his ground.

"Things just kept on getting worse, and an awful lot of bad luck settled on poor Hank. When he came back to Dr. Clark's house later that evening, he found out that Victor had accused him of stealing the ring. Dr. Clark was angry with Hank and forced him to return the ring before firing him.

"Victor left soon after to go back to Indian Territory, and the townsfolk were so deluded that they were sorry to see him go.

"Hank had no job and no money, and so with winter setting in, he knew that the only thing he could do was find Victor so he could be repaid for his doctoring services. The weather was cruel, but somehow Hank managed to track the trader. He was deathly sick when he finally found Victor, but the latter was as hard-hearted as ever. He refused to believe that he had ruined Hank's life, and, moreover, he claimed not to have the money to repay the debt.

"Anyway, Hank ended up dying miserably that winter, but Victor continued stopping over in the little town of Patience to sell his goods. A few of Hank's siblings came back to the town, and it was Hank's older brother Haggai who took up the fight over the ruby ring. Eventually, when Victor saw there was no way out of it, he gave in and sold the ring—at a profit, I assure you.

"Some time later, Victor again wanted the ring back. When Haggai refused to part with it, Victor set him up for a crime and got him arrested.

When Haggai finally got out of prison, he still wouldn't sell the ring back to Victor, so the two-faced trader shot him and took it. He stood trial but was so slippery that he managed to get away. That's all I know, but that's the story exactly as my grandfather would've told it."

Mr. Larone nodded as his last words died away.

The boys looked thoughtfully at him as the story's end brought them all back to reality.

Phil was the first to speak. "Er, could you please explain how Haggai knew all of the story, even though he wasn't there when Hank was alive?"

"He heard it from the townsfolk," Mr. Larone replied confidently. "But I think I forgot to mention that Hank got so ill that Victor had no choice but to take him back to Patience. Haggai chanced to meet them on the road. He would've heard some parts of the story from Hank first-hand before he passed away."

"Do you have any evidence to back up your claim to the ring, other than the story, that is?" Phil asked.

"Like what?" Mr. Larone frowned, evidently nettled by this question.

"Well, do you know what the ring looks like?"

Mr. Larone paused, a sly expression coming over his face. "Well yes, but I haven't finished. My grandfather knew the tale of our ancestors, and though the real ring had been lost in the mists of time, he decided to make a replica for his wife's birthday. It was gold, with a bright ruby, and beautifully delicate ornamentation."

Mr. Larone hesitated. "Uh . . . she loved it and wore it all the time . . . uh . . . until—until one of Victor James's descendants saw it and claimed it was the original one the families had fought over. Knowing the James's legacy of greed, my grandmother had no choice but to hide it amongst bottles of alcohol in the cellar in 1919."

Phil looked amazed at the new development of the story and the way it all started to make sense.

"Could you please tell us the meaning of the inscription on the back?" Andy asked curiously.

Seth nodded. "It's had us pretty puzzled."

"The inscription?" Mr. Larone frowned. It was awhile before he answered. "It's a bit of Latin nonsense, isn't it? I don't know."

Phil nodded. "Well, thank you for your time, Mr. Larone. We won't keep you any longer."

"Uh," Mr. Larone stammered, quickly rising from his chair, "what about that ring? It rightly belongs to me. Where exactly did you find it?"

"By the foundations of the old stables in the northernmost field of the farm. We understand how you feel, but our parents have to hear the story first."

Mr. Larone led the boys to the door, civilly shaking hands with each one. "You have my number, don't you?" he asked. "And you will let me know if I can help you or answer any more questions?"

"Thank you. I will bear that in mind."

As Phil drove home, Andy said, "Now that was an interesting visit."

"It certainly was," Phil agreed. "The heart is deceitful above all things. We can all learn a lesson by watching people change their behavior to try to get what they want. I'm glad Mr. Davis warned us about his character."

Seth nodded. "In Mr. Larone's story, that so-called missionary was quite awful, wasn't he?"

"Well, yes, the way he was portrayed was terrible, but certain details of that story leave me confused," Phil said.

"I agree. Some things just didn't make sense." Andy shook his head. "Why would a man give away a valuable ring and then ask for it back again?"

Seth frowned. "Those James people sound really nasty. Do you think there might be some of their descendants around today?"

Andy shrugged. "Maybe."

"Yes," Phil said slowly. "I wonder how different their story would sound. When we get home, I'm going to call Mr. Davis and ask if he's ever heard of the story Mr. Larone told. Then I'm going to ask him if he knows of people called the Jameses."

"You're brave, Phil," Seth said. "If it was me, I wouldn't want anything to do with those people."

Phil shook his head. "It wouldn't be just to accept one side of a story without any evidence. We know the Larone position, but we can't stop there."

****

"Hello, this is Vanessa speaking."

"Hello," Phil replied into the receiver later that day. "I'm looking for Mr. Matthew James. Is this the right number?"

"Yes, it is. One moment, please."

There was a shuffling sound as the receiver on the other end changed hands, and then an aged voice spoke. "Hello, this is Matthew."

"Good day, I'm Philip Baker. I got your number from Mr. George Davis because I'm busy researching the life story of Victor James, and I understand you're his descendant. Is that right?"

"That is correct. How can I help you?"

"Well, I heard someone tell a story involving Victor and thought it would be a good idea to contact you and compare the details. Could we please arrange to meet sometime?"

"Yes, of course. Would you like to come over to our house, say, tomorrow evening?"

"That sounds great. I look forward to it."

"Uh, I'm curious to know who told you the story about Victor," Matthew James said. "It wasn't Bud Larone, was it?"

CHAPTER 6

The next day was Saturday, and the Wilbur children came over to work on the film, riding their horses up the Bakers' front driveway early in the afternoon.

"Hey guys," they called.

"Hello," the Baker children responded.

"I'm really glad we're able to continue filming today," Emily said.

"We can do a re-take of the forest chase with our horses and get all those in-between parts we haven't filmed yet," Phil said.

"And we've made a picnic to take with us," Abby added.

"Then what are we waiting for?" Seth drawled with a grin. "Let's roll!"

****

The girl tightened her grip on the reins as her black horse plunged through the woods. The animal lengthened his stride at her urging, but his nostrils flared and he began to pant hard. Trees and logs whipped past, and forest creatures fled at the sound of the thundering hooves. The girl glanced backwards. Juan was gaining on her.

She looked down at her tiring mount, and knew that fleeing would be pointless. In a quick, brave motion, she turned her horse to face the enemy and clumsily drew a pistol from her belt. The other rider yanked his horse to a sudden stop, and the two faced each other tensely.

A grim smile wrinkled the corners of the cowboy's eyes. "Ooh, you've got a gun. I'm real scared now."

The girl pulled her lips into a tight line. "Don't move. I know you're out of powder, and I—I know how to use this."

"Sure ya do. Jus' like I know how to fly. Now gimme the gold."

The girl swallowed hard and frowned. "But—but I've got you covered. Don't move and I'll let you live."

"That's enough foolin' around. Hand over the gold."

"I can't. It's not mine to give."

A moment passed in silence. Then, suddenly, the cowboy flung himself to the ground and grabbed the pistol from the girl's hands, wrenching her from the saddle at the same time.

She shrieked in fright and kicked out as the cowboy snatched the bag of coins from her pocket. He pointed the gun at her with a savage snarl.

"Now get up. You're comin' with me."

The girl's eyes filled with terror, and she fainted as a sharp report rang out. The cowboy spun around angrily and a flash of brown, four-legged lightning streaked by. The horse skidded to a halt, and a young man leaped from its back, one gun in each hand.

"Leave my sister alone, coward!" he bellowed.

"Shoulda known you'd be on my tail, Fred."

"Juan, hand over the stolen gold. I'm gonna escort you to—"

"Save yer breath! I ain't going nowhere with you unless I'm dead! Duel." Juan raised the gun in his hands with a scowl.

Fred's sandy-colored eyebrows lowered beneath the line of his Stetson. "You know perfectly well that—"

The villain pulled the trigger, but nothing happened. In a frenzy, he leaped forward to attack, catching Fred off guard. The two cowboys were sent sprawling in the dust, rolling and wrestling madly. Fred dropped one gun and Juan snatched away the other. He was about to use it when Fred hurled his weight forward and knocked the villain unconscious with a powerful punch.

Fred retrieved his guns quickly, breathing hard and keeping one eye fixed on his enemy. The girl was starting to come round, and Fred was by her side in an instant.

"Brother! You did it!" she managed to say, sitting up. "You saved my life and recovered the gold."

Fred shakily returned his sister's embrace. "Yes, Annie, thank the Lord that's true. We're each bound by duty. I'm glad I had the grace to fulfill mine." He paused to glance at Juan's unmoving form, and then frowned. "What happened to your gun? How did he get it, and why didn't it fire?"

A slow smile spread over the girl's face. "Wa-al, a gun don't shoot if it ain't loaded."

"It wasn't loaded!"

Annie's eyes shone. "Nope. I forgot to."

There was a pause as her words sank in, and then a call of, "Cut! That was brilliant!"

Once Phil was certain they had all the shots, angles, and close-ups they needed, they all headed out of the forest, leading their horses to the large tree beside the river, which was the Bakers' customary picnic spot. They unsaddled the horses and tethered them nearby, and then sat on the grass and opened the backpacks containing their provisions of thick beef sandwiches and juice.

Later, once they had changed out of their costumes, Phil followed the directions he had been given and pulled up outside the James house. Matthew James, almost seventy and slightly stooped, eagerly invited him and the twins inside. They were led into the living room, where Matthew's wife, Vanessa, soon appeared carrying glasses of homemade lemonade.

"So Bud Larone told you his side of the story regarding Victor—and Haggai, no doubt," Mr. James said.

"That's right." Phil nodded and sipped the deliciously cool and sweet liquid.

"Well, I can already tell you that I'm grateful you've asked to hear our side, too," Mr. James replied. His face was creased around his eyes and mouth in such a way that it evidenced a man who was often joyful.

"Do you know Mr. Larone well?" Phil asked.

Mr. James swallowed some lemonade before nodding slowly, his features saddening. "Bud and I were at school together, we lived in the same town, and attended the same church. Our two families go back a long way, as you probably already know."

"Yes, sir."

"Our families first became acquainted way back in the days of the western frontier. Victor James was a young trader and missionary to the Indians, just like his father before him, and on one trip he decided to stop over at the little town of Patience for the first time.

"He caught a dose of 'flu on the way there, and arrived the same night that a dreadful rainstorm hit the town. Hank Larone, the doctor's apprentice, happened to see the wagon come slowly down the road, and he and the doctor brought Victor in and nursed him back to health.

"He didn't have any money to repay them, but he promised to do so once he had sold some of his goods in town. He was well enough to leave the doctor two days later, and planned to head for the pastor's house. As he was hitching his horse to the wagon, Hank approached him and asked for some kind of security to ensure that Victor paid his debt. Victor did not like this idea, but Hank was very manipulative, stressing the fact that he had effectually saved Victor's life. The situation was beginning to get unpleasant, so Victor finally agreed. He was about to hand over a fine buffalo hide when Hank spotted a valuable golden ring and demanded that instead.

"Victor at first refused, as it was a family heirloom, but Hank pressed so hard that Victor finally gave in. After all, Hank convinced him it would just be a security until he paid the debt.

"Victor headed to the home of the pastor, who knew Victor's father well. The pastor was thrilled to hear all about Victor's travels and successful missionary work with the Indians. The young man was so well-versed in Scripture and such a good speaker that the pastor decided the town could do with hearing him talk that Sunday.

"Victor was excited at this opportunity, and he prepared to speak about humility and forgiveness. When he did so, he didn't realize that it was a word extremely applicable to Hank, who became offended.

"All the churchgoers attended the big feast held after church at the pastor's house, including several important town figures. Many of them and their families had loved hearing Victor, and they thanked him for his words. I understand that this only heightened Hank's hostile sentiment, as he got jealous of Victor's popularity.

"Victor started selling his Indian goods from his wagon the next day. The townsfolk first visited his wagon out of curiosity, but soon simply out of the quality and value of his wares. He soon had enough cash to repay Hank and Dr. Clark, and offered to do so when Hank came to the wagon that evening. But Hank refused the money, claiming that Victor had given the ring away.

"Understandably, Victor was filled with righteous anger, and after unsuccessfully trying to get the ring back from Hank, went straight to Dr. Clark and explained the situation. The doctor was furious, and when Hank returned later, he demanded that the ring be given back.

"The time then came for Victor to leave town again and head back to Indian land, but Hank could not let go of anything that had happened to embarrass him. He had always been a volatile sort, but after Victor left, he turned so outwardly bitter, hostile, and cynical, that he could no longer be any good as a doctor and Dr. Clark had no choice but to fire him. My understanding is that this man was boiling over with hatred, blaming everything on Victor, and determining to make it his personal mission to destroy the trader.

"Now, you might think I'm just being harsh on Hank because I'm a James descendant, but that's not true. If you're going to get an understanding of the story, you have to know some background history. Hank's mother died when he was a young boy, and his father was a drunken layabout. The whole family lacked moral fiber, and that was what the town pastor tried to remedy by welcoming the children with open arms and teaching them as much as he could. That was cut short for the older children, because they left town when their father fled the punishment of stealing. Hank was left behind, however, and no matter how much time was spent in trying to nurture him, he had a deeply-rooted bitterness in his heart that did not go away. By the time Victor came to town, it only needed a little prodding to flower into hostility and even hatred. Dr. Clark would have known Hank extremely well, and was something of a father-figure to him, so the fact that he forced Hank to give the ring back is proof that Hank had serious character flaws.

"Anyway, winter was setting in, but Hank decided to go after Victor anyway, trying to track him into Indian land. He followed the trail until he finally caught up and found Victor's camp, but by then he had caught something serious—it may have been pneumonia. Victor nursed him as well as he could, but soon decided to take Hank back to Patience. When they were nearing the town, they happened to meet Hank's older brother Haggai on the road. I assume this gave Haggai the chance to hear what had happened from Hank's own perspective, because just after he died, Haggai began to badger Victor about the gold ring.

"This is where the James record and the Larone record differ the most. The story as it passed down our family is that Haggai stole the ring from Victor and became an outlaw, like his father before him.

"Just as all outlaws come to justice in some way, Haggai eventually did, too. He was caught in another town for another crime, and was taken to prison. Victor, by then a married and older man, came to demand the ring that was stolen from him, but Haggai denied the accusation and refused to tell where he had hidden it.

"When Haggai's prison term was completed, he still had not revealed the whereabouts of the ring. He went home to his wife and children, but could not escape his bad habits and returned to fleeing from the law, eventually being shot by a rival outlaw gang. The story that was passed down Haggai's family, though, is that he bought the ring from Victor, and wouldn't give it back when Victor changed his mind about it." Matthew James sighed. "They even accused Victor of shooting Haggai out of malice. Though Victor stood trial, and was found innocent, Haggai's family did not stop spreading the slander, and it has continued down the generations."

Phil and the twins didn't reply for some time.

"That's quite a story," Abby said finally.

Phil nodded. "It all makes sense now. Do you happen to know anything about a replica ring that was made by Mr. Bud Larone's grandfather?"

Mr. James frowned. "No, not much. When Bud was a boy, he used to mention things about archeology and buried treasure, but he was firmly scolded for it and became very secretive about the topic."

Phil quickly told the man what Mr. Larone had said about the replica needing to be hidden from James greed, and Mr. James was indignant. "That's nonsense! Why, I have *never* heard any of that before!"

Phil shifted in his seat. "I think we can all agree that it's time to tell you about the ring we found."

With that, they proceeded to tell the gentleman all about the ring's discovery. By the end he was blinking with excitement.

"That must be the one that's been lost for generations!" he exclaimed. "It's finally been found! I can tell you all about that ring. My grandfather thought it was an important piece of family history, as it was passed down the generations until Haggai took it, so he tried to trace its story. I've got his discoveries in this book here."

He fetched from the bookshelf an old, leather volume, and laid it open on his knees as he sat down again.

"We think the ring was first made in England by a tiny jewelery shop. It was purchased there by our ancestors, who then immigrated here, to America, to join the young colonies. As time passed, the family tradition was that the ring would be passed down to the oldest son who married, and kept by his wife. This here is a copy of a diary entry belonging to one such wife. 'The ring is a pretty little thing of great value to this family. The gold is of fine quality, the ruby shines brilliantly, and everybody who sees it admires the intricate metalwork.'

"Here is a drawing someone made of it," he said, tapping his finger on a large, detailed illustration.

They studied it for some time. Then Mr. James went paging on through the book, but Phil found it difficult to concentrate with all the thoughts that whirled around in his mind. Only when Mr. James mentioned Victor could he again pay attention.

"After Haggai was shot, Victor knew there would be no hope of ever finding the ring unless Haggai's wife and son Barnaby had some idea where he might have put it. Victor traveled to wherever it was they lived, but they insisted that Haggai had not even mentioned a ring. It has been lost ever since."

The drive home was characterized by thoughtful silence punctuated by spurts of conversation.

"That was a beautiful drawing," Abby said, "but one thing jumped out at me. Though there was an interesting symbol inside the band, there was no inscription."

"That could have been made after the drawing was completed," Phil said.

"I wonder which ring we found," Andy said. "It could be the replica that Mr. Larone spoke about, or it could be the original. I certainly was astounded at all the information Mr. James had about that original ring."

"And his story made a lot more sense," Phil agreed. "Mr. Larone made some strong accusations against the James family, including unproven murder."

"That doesn't mean that all his details were wrong." Abby paused for a moment. "But I do think it's much more likely that Mr. James has his facts straight. He and his wife were lovely."

"Yes," Phil agreed. "I'm glad we decided to check up on their side of the story."

"As far as I can see, there's only one way we can prove for a fact who is right," Andy said, "and that's by getting the ring dated."

CHAPTER 7

The phone rang on Monday evening, and Phil answered to find Mr. Wilbur on the other end of the line. Phil and the twins had already conveyed to him the results of their visit two days before.

"Hello Phil, is your dad home?"

"He's down in the workshop. Shall I call him?" Phil couldn't help noticing the tightness in Mr. Wilbur's voice, and wondered what was wrong.

"Yes, please."

Phil hurried out to the workshop, his mind racing. Mr. Wilbur was much too strained. Something was wrong. What could it be?

Mr. Baker picked up the phone in his workshop, and Phil went back inside to replace the receiver he'd put on the counter's surface. He tried to focus on his studies again, but his concentration was shattered. He hoped the news wasn't too bad. The more he tried to avoid being distracted, the more often he glanced at the clock, its second hand ticking slower as time passed. *Perhaps it's nothing to worry about*, Phil reasoned. *Maybe the call has to do with the car needing repairs, or a fence needing fixing, or . . .*

"Alice! Phil!"

The interrupting calls came from Mr. Baker, at the back door. Phil needed no further encouragement. He shot out of his seat and flew down the stairs. Mrs. Baker was appearing from the corridor, her expression one of surprise.

"What is it, dear?"

"It's Jed. He's got some bad news."

"What's it about?" Phil asked breathlessly.

"This afternoon he was going to take the ring to the jeweler to get it polished and dated—but he can't find it!"

"Oh, no! Should we help him look?" Mrs. Baker asked.

"I offered, but he said they'd already searched the entire house."

"So the ring is lost?" Phil muttered incredulously.

"That's the thing," Mr. Baker replied, his voice deep with tension. "It might have been stolen."

Mrs. Baker made no sound, but her face spoke volumes.

"Is that possible?" Phil frowned.

"It was last in Jed's study. They've searched it from top to bottom."

Mrs. Baker let out a long breath. "If it really was stolen, what was the reason? It can't have been that valuable, could it?"

"I don't know," Mr. Baker replied.

Phil looked shocked. "This is bad news, but the Lord has taken our family through many tight spots before."

"You're right," Mr. Baker agreed. "We need to trust Him. And find out what's going on."

Mr. Baker and Phil arrived at the Wilburs' house a little later to find two police cars in the driveway. They headed inside and answered the questions the police put to them, explaining the whole story of the crates and discovery of the ring.

"That's a fascinating story," one of the men said.

Then Phil asked, "How could a thief get in?"

"Most probably through the window," the officer answered. "Jed said he might have left it ajar during the night. A thief could have brought a ladder, or might have been practiced at climbing walls."

When Phil and Mr. Baker got home, the smell of Chinese stir-fry wafted from the kitchen and the children were just finished setting the table for supper. Mr. Baker told them about the police questioning as they sat down to eat.

"Do you think the thief will be caught?" Mrs. Baker asked.

Her husband paused, trying to secure a mound of stir-fry with his chopsticks. "I don't know. The police examined the room for fingerprints, but didn't find any belonging to a stranger."

He gave a sigh of annoyance as for the third time his noodles slipped back into his bowl. "Abby, please get me a knife and fork—I can't eat with my fingers on stilts."

Andy laughed. "I agree! It would almost be easier to use a straw than these."

"A straw! I want to use a straw!" Tom exclaimed. "Oh Mother, Father, can I use one? Please?"

"Not unless you want your supper blended into a smoothie," Mrs. Baker replied with a twinkle in her eye.

As Abby jumped up to head for the kitchen, Phil was frowning in thought.

"Father, who would have done such a thing? Only Mr. James and Mr. Larone have strong enough motives to arrange something so drastic."

"Besides, the newspaper only came out this morning," Mr. Baker added. "If the ring was stolen during the night, which is most probable, no criminal would have read of its discovery yet."

Andy's eyes widened. "Of course! So our suspects narrow down to just two men."

"But which of them would resort to theft?" Mrs. Baker asked.

"Mr. Larone is much more of a likely candidate than Mr. James," Abby said as she returned.

"By far!" Andy agreed.

Mr. Baker was thoughtful. "It's risky for both of them. After all, if either was caught arranging the theft, he'd be in big trouble and might even lose his claim to the ring."

"It must have been Mr. Larone," Abby said. "Mr. James sounds really sincere."

"I agree, but since the ring is gone, it can't be dated and we can't know whose story is true," Phil pointed out. "The one whose story is false must have stolen it, because he knows he won't get it any other way. Mr. James was indignant when he heard what Mr. Larone said; maybe he felt he couldn't prove his story."

Andy frowned. "Are you saying Mr. James's story might not be true?"

"Well . . . not exactly, but . . ."

"Look, we really don't know," Mr. Baker said, trying to stem the tide of flurrying thoughts and questions. "We can't accuse either man of something so extreme without a scrap of proof. 'You shall do no injustice in judgment,' from Leviticus 19, remember?"

The children nodded. That was part of a verse they'd memorized.

"We have to get to the bottom of this," Mr. Baker continued, "but to do so we're going to need facts."

****

The next day was Thursday, and that afternoon Abby headed over to the Wilbur farm to go on a ride with Emily. The girl was down at the stables, just finished tacking Cappuccino up.

"Hey, Emily," Abby greeted.

Emily straightened up. "Hi."

"Did you hear about our most recent considerations?"

Emily nodded. "It must have been one of those two men. Maybe they should both be arrested until we find out which is guilty" She heaved herself into the saddle.

Abby laughed. "That would certainly be convenient, but not very just."

"Thieving isn't very just," Emily countered as they left the stables.

"I know," Abby said, "but we can't accuse anybody without evidence—or else we'd be in the wrong."

Emily sighed. "I guess you're right. I really wanted that ring."

Abby thought for a moment, and then a smile lit up her hazel eyes. "I'll race you to that fence!" So saying, she squeezed her heels into Arrow's sides. He seemed to pause, as if wondering whether or not Abby was serious, and then leaped into a canter.

Emily was taken by surprise, but Cappuccino followed at a trot and needed little urging to pursue the diminishing figures. The fence was a considerable distance away, and by the time the competing horses neared it, they were showing signs of fatigue.

"You win," Emily puffed as she slowed Cappuccino to a trot.

Abby laughed, patting Arrow's neck. She was sure the sudden rush had helped to clear her friend's head. Both girls' faces were flushed from the exhilarating ride, and they proceeded at a leisurely walk.

"Hmm," Emily muttered once she had caught her breath a little. "What about that detective you're always talking about—Detective Mordecai, isn't it? Didn't he help you with that mystery in England? Do you think he could help?"

"Detective Mortimer—yes, we already thought of him. Unfortunately, he's busy with another case, but he said he'd be glad to help us once he's done if we haven't already figured it all out by then."

"That's not likely."

They rode on and chatted for some time, until Abby stopped with a frown. "Look—tire tracks," she said, pointing to the soft ground.

"That's strange," Emily said. "I don't think my dad's been down here with the tractor yet."

"Those don't look like tractor marks. Maybe your father drove his car down here while you were busy doing schoolwork."

Emily shrugged. "Hey, we'd better hurry up or I won't have all my chores done before supper."

When they arrived back at the house, Abby noticed Mrs. Wilbur looking unusually strained.

"Are you all right, Mrs. Wilbur?" she asked as she was about to turn Arrow for home.

The lady attempted a smile. "Thank you, Abby, I'm fine. It's just that all this stress is getting to me. The upheaval of moving, the snake, the missing ring, and confusing stories about the wild west—I just can't wait for things to get back to normal."

Once Abby got home, Mrs. Baker and she headed to the grocery store. Since Andy wanted to buy himself a new memory card for his camera, he had come along too. They were in the frozen food aisle when Andy whispered, "Here comes Mr. Larone."

Mrs. Baker turned around just in time to see the man approach them.

"Andy, what a surprise to see you here," Mr. Larone said with an oily smile.

"Hello, Mr. Larone," Andy replied. "This is my mother, Mrs. Baker, and my sister, Abigail."

"Pleased to meet you both. I'm Bud. I've been wondering how you've been getting on with tracing the owner of that ring you found."

"Oh, we have quite a few other matters to concentrate on," Mrs. Baker answered.

The man frowned. "Do you mean to say you've given up? Aren't you going to find out more about it?"

Mrs. Baker smiled politely, glancing at the twins quickly to request their silence. "We're doing the best we can."

Bud nodded and seemed to quieten down. He looked either way, and then leaned forward. "I just want to warn you to keep that ring in a safe place until I can prove I'm the rightful owner. I saw the article in the newspaper, and want to tell you that there will be a fair bit of hoo-ha when Matthew James hears about it. He used to be a mountaineer, and the perseverance that drove him on hasn't weakened with age, if you catch my meaning."

His eyes wandered down the aisle, then they were riveted by something and his face hardened. "It was a pleasure talking to you," he said abruptly, pulling his eyes back to Mrs. Baker and the twins. "Send my regards to your family." Quickly, he turned and walked away.

Abby glanced behind her, wondering what could have disturbed the man. She could see nothing but food items and other shoppers.

"That was a strange conversation," she said softly.

Just then an aged lady came up to them, a bag of mixed vegetables in her hand. "I'm sorry to bother you, but I left my glasses at home. Could one of you please read this and tell me the ingredients?"

"Yes, of course," Abby responded, looking up at the lady. As she did so, her lips parted. "Mrs. James!"

The lady looked at Abby for a moment before recognition spread over her face. "Oh yes, of course! You and your brothers came to visit a few days ago."

"Yes, that's right." Abby nodded. "This is my mother, Mrs. Alice Baker. Mother, this is Mrs. Vanessa James."

"Pleased to meet you," Mrs. Baker responded, her manners ever ready.

"And you, too," Vanessa said. "Your children are wonderfully polite. The fair-haired young man—is he your eldest?"

"Phil? Yes, he is."

"Matthew kept on remarking how respectful he was."

"I'm glad to hear that."

Once Abby had read off the list of vegetables in the packet, the lady thanked her and said, "We saw the article in the paper—have you got many responses?"

"It was our friend Jed Wilbur who wrote the article. He hasn't told us about any responses yet," Mrs. Baker replied.

Vanessa nodded. "Well, that ring is all Matthew has been able to talk about these last few days. He'd love to see it."

Mrs. Baker's smile froze in place as she considered what to say. "I'm sure he would. The Wilbur family is pretty busy at the moment. Now is probably not a good time to ask."

"Oh, all right," Vanessa said, a little surprised, but understanding. "Well, it was good to meet you. I hope everything can be settled soon."

Mrs. Baker and the twins returned home deep in thought. Supper was quickly prepared and then they told the story to Mr. Baker and Phil, trying not to leave out a single detail.

"Mr. Larone was trying to warn us about Mr. James by implying bad character," Andy said afterward.

"Did you notice Mr. Larone stare at something before disappearing?" Abby asked.

"I did," Mrs. Baker said.

"It can only have been Mrs. James that disturbed him," Abby continued. "I don't think anything else could get that kind of reaction from him."

"Yes," Mrs. Baker agreed with a slow nod. "Yes, I think you're right."

"It's a pity that Detective Mortimer is busy," Phil said.

The others muttered their agreement, knowing that solving the mystery would take far longer alone.

CHAPTER 8

When Abby came into the living room much later, she found Phil and Andy in conversation with her parents. She could not help noticing that her parents looked like they had some news.

"Ah, Abby; you're just in time," her father said. "Your mother and I wanted to tell you three about a recent development."

Abby waited curiously.

"Since Jed lost the ring, both Bud and Matthew have actually contacted him to arrange to see it. Jed asked the police what to do, as telling the two men that it's been stolen might not be wise."

"Why not?" Andy asked.

"Well, all we know for sure is that it's missing. We can't prove it was stolen," Mr. Baker explained. "If we let on that we suspect one of them as a thief, that might alarm the guilty one into handing the ring over to an accomplice so we'd never find it. The longer we can keep the guilty person calm and unsuspecting, the better chance we have of catching him."

"I see." Andy nodded.

"Jed and Hannah are both going to be busy, and we thought that you could take care of the children. Think of something you can do to take their minds off things."

"I wouldn't know what to suggest other than playing games," Abby said. "To be honest, I've been thinking about this case a lot myself."

"Me too," Phil nodded. "My creativity levels are running low."

"Well," Andy began, glancing at his siblings, "we could finish that film we were making."

"Great idea!" Mrs. Baker encouraged. "That would be perfect. Why not get started tomorrow?"

The next morning, Abby called the Wilbur house to share the idea of filming the last scenes of their movie. Mrs. Wilbur was very keen on the idea, as it would free up some of her time, and said that the kids would ride over in one hour's time.

While she waited, Abby surveyed the costumes she and Emily had worked on. A few years before, Mrs. Baker had stumbled across an old, wooden dress-up box in an antique store, and it had been full of all sorts of detailed historical costumes. She had purchased it, thinking that the children would certainly find use for the items. There were spurs, neckerchiefs, Stetsons, and cowboyish waistcoats, as well as many things the children had not needed for their film—a black cloak, a feathered hat, bonnets, fans, a parasol, and several dresses trimmed with ruffles and beads.

When the Wilbur children arrived, the Bakers welcomed them jovially, unable to help noticing the gloomy tinge to their friends' faces.

"Is something the matter?" Abby asked Emily.

"Oh, nothing much. It's just that the police seem to have got the idea that my dad might have hidden the ring so he could keep it."

"But that's outrageous!" Andy burst out. "It was your father who advertised it in the first place!"

Seth shrugged. "I know."

"Probably they don't suspect your father," Phil pointed out, "but they have to consider all possibilities, especially since Mr. Larone and Mr. James have been eager to claim the ring."

"Yeah. My parents have been pretty stressed," Emily said.

"Here, Seth," Abby said, holding out one of the waistcoats she had been adjusting. "This is the extra one. I need you to try it on for size, please, but mind the pins!"

"Emily, look at this crown we bought," Tom said, raising his big, blue eyes to meet her green ones.

"Hmm, that looks good," she replied in a monotone.

Abby cast a glance at Phil and Andy. They were all thinking the same thing: *Cheer up the Wilburs!*

"Er, ahem," Phil cleared his throat quickly, "I'm just going to fetch two pairs of boots that need a polish. I won't be long."

Soon after, Andy went out to fetch the camera equipment, leaving the Wilbur children with Abby and Tom.

Abby noticed Seth struggling to fit into the waistcoat he was trying on. She motioned for Emily to help, and the two of them began adjusting the pins so it fit better.

"Ouch!" Seth burst out, turning on Emily. "You pricked me on purpose!"

Abby started back in surprise at the outburst, and Tom looked up with wide eyes.

"Did not!" Emily retorted. "It's your fault—if you didn't eat so much this wouldn't be as tight!"

Abby gulped. *What should I do?* she thought frantically. *Jesus wouldn't want siblings to fight like this. I know I should say something, but what? I dare not offend E—wait, it's not that—I just don't want to take sides,* she tried to persuade herself. *Yes, I don't want to take sides.*

"Hey!" Seth cried. "You know what Mom has said about that! You're not allowed to tease me!"

"I wasn't teasing—I was telling the truth!"

"The truth?" Seth fumed. "You're—"

"Hey! 'The beginning of strife is like releasing water,'" said a commanding voice from the doorway. It was Phil. "'Therefore stop contention before a quarrel starts.'"

The silence that came at that moment was almost as deafening as the angry cries that had preceded it. Abby was frozen in her posture of shock, one pin balancing in her fingers. Tom was still staring at the scene.

"You don't understand, Phil," Seth finally muttered. "You couldn't."

"Oh, I understand strife, all right."

"No, I mean that thing you said about quarrels."

"That was Proverbs 17:14."

There was an awkward pause.

Abby had a sickening feeling in the pit of her stomach. She couldn't look Phil in the eye.

Mrs. Baker came to the door awhile afterward, carrying a tray of freshly-baked cookies and mugs of hot chocolate. She returned some time later to call Emily to the phone. By then, almost all the preparations had been made to begin filming.

Emily rushed back into the room. "That was Mom on the phone. She said we need to come home right away—she forgot about taking us to piano lessons and we're going to be late!"

The Wilburs scrambled to pack away their things as quickly as they could.

"I guess we can film that last scene some other time," Abby said, quite relieved that there would be no more outbursts to deal with for the rest of the day.

"Yes." Emily nodded. "Mom says maybe tomorrow we'll be at a loose end again."

The Wilburs raced down to the paddock, where they had left their horses, tacked up, and rode off within ten minutes.

"Are you all right, Abby?" Phil asked as they all walked back up to the house.

"Yes, you're looking a bit pale," Andy added as he glanced her way.

"Oh, er," she stammered, "I'm just a little shaken, that's all."

"By the squabble?" Phil asked.

Abby nodded.

"Yes, well, strife is ugly," Phil said. "I suppose that's why we're told, 'Blessed are the peacemakers.'"

Abby's stomach did a somersault, and she was surprised she didn't look seasick instead of slightly pale.

"Peacemakers," she repeated with a little nod. Secretly she thought, *There's no way I could ever be one of those.*

At lunch, the Bakers spoke about the events that had been consuming their attention for the last few days. Mr. Baker came up from his workshop to join the meal.

"I've been wondering if there's a reason both Mr. Larone and Mr. James are suddenly both so eager to see the ring," Phil said.

"Probably they each know the other is after it," Mrs. Baker suggested, "and neither wants to lose out on a family heirloom."

"I wonder if we'll ever know whether the ring is really stolen, or just lost," Abby said. She sighed.

"Well, what did the police say?" Phil asked, trying to think back to their last visit to the Wilbur house.

"Hey!" Andy suddenly cried. "Didn't the officer say the thief probably came in through the upstairs window?"

"Yes," Phil replied. "What about it?"

"When Mr. Larone spoke to us at the store, he said that Mr. James still had the perseverance of his younger days—"

"When he was a mountaineer!" Abby finished.

Both Mr. and Mrs. Baker looked taken aback. Phil was frowning.

"Look," Mrs. Baker said, regaining composure first, "a mountaineer doesn't automatically qualify as a cat burglar. I would have thought Mr. James a little old for that sort of thing, anyway."

"He might know cat burglars from his mountaineering experience," Andy suggested.

"Cat burglars?" Tom repeated, his small forehead creased. "Why would Mr. James want to steal cats?"

Abby laughed. "No, no—cat burglars don't have anything to do with cats. They're thieves who enter buildings by climbing up and getting in through windows of upper stories."

"Bud's comment does give us something to work with. Either Matthew is responsible for stealing the ring," Mr. Baker spoke, his words rolling as fast as his thoughts, "or Bud arranged the theft and thus knows how to incriminate Matthew."

"There are still two options," Abby frowned. "Always another mystery."

After lunch, Phil and Mr. Baker needed to pick up some materials from the hardware store for the invention they were busy on, so they jumped into the car and drove to town.

They had purchased all the goods they needed and loaded them into the car, when Phil suddenly pointed. "Look. There's Mr. Larone—and he's carrying a little spade! What could he be up to?"

"I don't know," Mr. Baker said with a frown. "I suppose we could watch."

They peered around the corner the man had just disappeared behind, and watched as he walked more and more cautiously out of town. They followed at a distance, and soon noticed he was heading straight for an area of grassy, open ground near deserted playground equipment. When he had glanced around stiffly, he began digging a hole beside a very large tree.

"What *is* he doing?" Phil muttered, straining his eyes to see from their distant vantage point.

Suddenly, there was a call behind them, and they swung around to see Mr. Davis walking in their direction.

"Hello there," was his friendly greeting. "What brings you to town at this time?"

"Why, hello," Mr. Baker responded. "We were just buying materials we need from the hardware store."

"Ah—do I hear the sound of another invention?"

Phil nodded. "We're working on one."

"And how about that ring?" Mr. Davis asked. "Did you manage to contact Matthew James after visiting Bud?"

"Yes, we did," Phil replied. "The stories don't agree, but they're both very interesting."

"I have no doubt about that. Anyway, it was good to see you. Please send my regards home."

Once Mr. Davis had shuffled away, Phil and Mr. Baker quickly turned back, remembering that they had been watching Mr. Larone. A group of mothers with small children was starting to congregate in the grassy area, and the kids were obviously going to make use of the swings and other playground equipment. Phil scanned the faces with a sinking heart. Mr. Larone was gone.

CHAPTER 9

Abby was busy completing her history assignment when there was a soft tap on the bedroom door.

"Come in," Abby answered, looking up from her desk.

Mrs. Baker's face appeared as the door opened, and she slipped inside the room, gently closing the door behind her.

"Abby, do you have a minute?"

"Yes, of course, Mother."

Mrs. Baker sat down in the comfortable reading chair near the desk. "Abby, Phil mentioned Emily and Seth's strife. I must have been outside when it happened because I didn't hear a thing. Phil said you were shaken up by it, and I wanted to ask how you're doing."

"Oh . . ." Abby thought for a moment. "I'm sure I'll be okay."

"What upset you the most about it?"

"Well," Abby began, "I suppose the suddenness of it shocked me, as well as the fact that there wasn't actually any reason for their fight. I felt that I should have said something, but what? There was nothing to say without taking sides."

"Taking sides?" Mrs. Baker repeated. "What did Phil say to stop them?"

"He quoted a Scripture."

"And did he face the dilemma of taking sides?"

"No." Abby shook her head.

"So now you'll know what to do for next time, won't you?" Mrs. Baker asked with a smile.

"Next time." Abby swallowed. "Yes."

Something in her daughter's tone kept Mrs. Baker from rising to leave. "Dear, I know it's hard to be something of a role-model to a friend who is older than you. Is that a part of your struggle?"

Abby looked down at her desk, then forced her eyes back up. "Yes, Mother."

"Was Emily's opinion the reason you were afraid to say anything?"

"Yes, I suppose so," Abby admitted. "I would never have guessed I'd struggle in this way. After all, cousin Millie is older than me, and I wasn't worried about her opinion when she came to visit."

Mrs. Baker almost laughed. "I don't think any of you children were worried about *that*! Emily is far sweeter and much more charming than your cousin was. It's generally the 'nice' people we have to keep ourselves from idolizing, not the selfish ones."

Abby sighed, knowing deep down that her mother was right.

"Dear, Emily may be athletic, fun-loving, and charming. And pretty," Mrs. Baker added, making Abby shift uncomfortably, "but those are not virtues the Bible holds up. There are many things she needs to learn—many things you can teach her if you have the courage and love. 'Open rebuke is better than love carefully concealed,' and 'faithful are the wounds of a friend,' right?"

Abby nodded. "Proverbs 27."

"What's more important: staying in Emily's 'good books' all the time, or lovingly helping her out of sin?"

"Helping her," Abby answered. "Mother, I know you're right, but I'm worried that I'll lose her friendship completely." Tears welled in her eyes.

Mrs. Baker put her hand on her daughter's arm. "You may lose a bit of favor for awhile, but you'll please God. In the end, you'll earn Emily's respect and she'll thank you for your faithfulness. That's far better than keeping quiet and having a pricked conscience all the time. And you know what? As you reach out in obedience to God, that will have a ripple effect on the people around you—even if you don't get to see it."

"Thank you, Mother," came Abby's muffled voice as Mrs. Baker embraced her in a motherly hug. "I needed that."

Just then they heard the front door open and bang shut, and they knew Mr. Baker and Phil had returned. Abby and her mother came downstairs as Andy and Tom appeared, and Mr. Baker quickly told the details of what they had witnessed in town.

"Mr. Larone was carrying a spade through town and then started digging a hole next to a tree? That sounds suspicious to me," Andy said.

Phil frowned. "But why, as Father said, was he going about in broad daylight if he was up to something bad? Why not wait for nightfall?"

"Maybe he needs light for whatever he's doing, and can't see so well in the dark," Tom suggested.

Phil nodded. "You have a point."

"Maybe we should go and investigate," Andy said. "This might have something to do with the ring."

"Exactly!" Abby nodded. "He may be hiding it there!"

"I really had planned to get some important work done," Mr. Baker said slowly, "but this might result in a clue. Phil, you know where we were. Have a look around, but be careful."

Phil drove the twins into town just as the sun was setting. The car pulled up on the grass near the tree and the three excited Bakers rushed out to examine the ground. Nobody was nearby.

"This is it," Phil said, pointing to a small patch of disturbed soil which had been disguised with a scattering of grass over it. "I'm sure this is where Mr. Larone was digging. He must have filled in the hole and tried to hide the lack of grass here."

He carefully set to work with his small hand-shovel, hoping not to damage anything that might be hidden beneath the soil. He dug for a few minutes without uncovering anything.

"That's strange," Abby said. "I was sure we were on to something."

"Maybe there was something hidden here which he found," Andy said.

Phil dug a little deeper, and then sighed. "I've struck one of the tree's roots. There's definitely nothing here." He started filling in the hole while the twins spread out and looked for indications of other places Mr. Larone might have dug.

Phil gasped. "Wait a second—look at this!"

He had upturned a small, plastic pouch containing a folded piece of paper. He hurriedly opened it. The paper was typed with the words: *Meet me here tomorrow, 3p.m.*

"Mr. Larone must be arranging to meet somebody here at that time!" Andy exclaimed.

"This must definitely be something sinister if he went to all that trouble to hide the note," Abby said.

"It sure seems that way," Phil agreed. "I'm going to put this back, so that whoever comes looking for it will find it. I think we should come tomorrow and see exactly what is going on."

The next day was busy as there were many farm and household chores to catch up on, but the thought that fueled each of the children to work quickly and diligently was that of discovering the meaning of the note Mr. Larone left.

"Who knows," Abby said to Andy, "maybe he has the ring and is going to pass it on to an accomplice."

But the afternoon brought disappointing news. "That was Mrs. Wilbur on the phone just then," Mrs. Baker said. "She asked us to look after the children. They hoped to continue filmmaking."

"Oh, Mother, we were planning to solve the mystery at three o'clock today," Andy said, feeling very deflated. "We won't be able to if the Wilburs are with us—there's not enough space in the car."

"I'm still going to watch that spot," Mr. Baker said, "and I can tell you everything that happens when I get back."

"Can't some of us go with you?" Abby asked hopefully.

Mr. Baker shook his head. "Not this time. I've got a feeling this could turn dangerous, and I'll look less suspicious in town by myself. Besides, aren't you all needed for filming to continue?"

Mr. and Mrs. Wilbur dropped their children off soon afterward, and the twins filled them in on their discovery the previous night.

"Wow," Seth said. "So your dad is going to be watching the place at three p.m.? That's exciting."

Emily nodded. "I hope we're still around when he comes back so we can hear about all that happens."

"Yes. Now, what about your horses?" Phil asked. "We need them for filming."

"Our parents said we could fetch them if we need to; we were just in too much of a hurry to bring them over earlier," Emily replied.

"Another thing we need to consider is the location of our final scene," Andy said. "We were talking about setting up on a large hill, but we don't have any that are suitable."

"We've got a great hill on our farm," Seth suggested. "Maybe we could use that."

"Would your parents mind?" Phil asked.

"Not at all!"

Quickly, Phil told Mrs. Baker their plan to take everything over to the Wilburs' farm and to film on the hill Seth had mentioned. She thought it was a good idea, so they tacked up four horses and packed all their equipment, decorations, and props into the car. Finally, before setting out, they all dressed in their costumes.

Phil was going to drive over to the farm with the younger children while the others rode there. They looked quite a dashing sight in their costumes, and Seth didn't hesitate to take photos.

Once at the farm, the Wilburs tacked up their own horses while the Bakers divided up the load from the car, intending to leave the vehicle in the driveway.

"I think we've got everything," Phil announced as he checked that the car was empty. Seth led the way to the hill he had mentioned, and the others agreed it would work perfectly for the scene.

"Are we going to set up at the top of the hill?" Abby asked, glancing at Phil.

Seth shook his head vigorously. "Oh, no—Phil, please don't say we have to do that. We'll save energy if we don't have to trudge all the way up and down all the time. There's even a perfect spot for the tripod down here in this dip."

They gathered half-way up the hill, setting up a makeshift camp while Seth polished his Sheriff badge and Andy adjusted the tripod. Abby, Emily, and Laura flapped a sheet and set it up as a tent, while the boys stacked logs as if for a fire. The horses stood grazing, their Western tack having been polished until it shone.

Since Andy and Emily weren't needed for the scene, they were both going to be filming it. Once everybody had been told what to do, Andy cried, "Three, two, one, action!" and started the camera.

Seth came cantering in on Geronimo and pulled up in the camp, jumping out of the saddle. "I'm lookin' fer Fred."

"I'm here, Sheriff Beans," Phil said, rising as he wiped his hands on his waistcoat. "Am I in trouble?"

"Trouble?" Seth chortled. "Anythin' but! Mr. Bonner put out a reward for Juan, sayin' that whoever caught the scoundrel could have half the recovered gold."

"Half?" Abby cried. "Why, that's a fortune!"

"This is fer you," Seth said, tossing a leather pouch to Phil.

Phil looked astounded. "That means we have enough to pay the bills! I'm goin' home right away to tell Mother."

He swung himself up into the saddle and turned his horse towards the top of the hill at a trot. He had just reached it when he suddenly stopped in his tracks. Andy was about to yell "Cut!" when he noticed his brother's behavior and watched intently. Phil backed the horse away and flung himself to the ground, staring over the top of the hill until Andy couldn't contain his curiosity any longer. He ran forward, putting his finger to his lips as he passed the others.

"Shhh! Something's up," he hissed, not slowing down.

The others, too, began rushing up the hill, and it was Phil's turn to quiet them in an urgent tone and signal for them to stay low.

Nothing could have prepared them for what they saw when they got to the top.

CHAPTER 10

I n the distance was a helicopter, its blades stationery, and beside it were a few men working quickly.

"What are they doing?" Emily whispered, her eyes wide. "This is our land!"

"I don't know," Phil replied grimly. "Whatever it is, I'm calling the police." He eased his iPhone from his pocket and began dialing the number.

The horses, which had suddenly been left unattended, began to wander and graze, and Geronimo came too close to the tripod and knocked it over. The sudden "thud" that resulted gave the animal a fright, and he cantered around the hill and straight into view of the men in the distance. He stopped a few strides later, but it was too late. Tom and Laura jumped up and rushed to retrieve the horse, despite their siblings' instructions to the contrary.

A glint of light caught Phil's eye, and he could just make out the form of one of the men peering in their direction through binoculars.

"They've seen us," Andy muttered grimly as he, too, saw the man quickly turn away and speak to his accomplices. Moments later, the blades of the helicopter started to whirl and the men hurried to finish what they were doing.

"Come on, Phil—let's ride over there before they get away!" Andy exclaimed.

Phil wrestled with the idea for awhile, struggling to make a decision. Then he shook his head.

"They are obviously doing something illegal and might be armed. We can't take that risk and leave the others by themselves. I'm supposed to be here to look after you all."

"The police!" Abby cried. "Did you get them?"

"No," Phil replied, suddenly remembering that his intention had been interrupted by Geronimo. By the time he had completed the call, the men were all inside the helicopter and it was slowly lifting off the ground.

"Aargh!" Andy groaned in frustration. "I can't believe they're getting away and there's nothing we can do about it!"

"We have to go investigate," Emily said. "We must find out what they were up to!"

They all mounted and dashed for the spot they had last seen the helicopter, Phil giving the condition that they were not allowed to touch anything.

"I think it was about here," Seth said as they neared the spot.

"There are the helicopter marks," Emily said, pointing to flattened grass.

"And here's a lot of disturbed ground," Phil added with a frown. "I'm going to call home now and tell Mother what happened. Maybe Father is home already."

Mrs. Baker was shocked to hear the news. She said that Mr. Baker was not yet back, and that the children should come home as soon as the police had no further need of them.

The police arrived a few minutes later, and all of the children were at the house to meet them. Phil grimaced when he realized they were still in costume, and hoped the police would take them seriously nevertheless.

"So let me get this straight," the policeman said. "You were busy filming when you looked over the hill and saw a helicopter in the distance and men working beside it?"

"That's right." Phil nodded.

"Well, let's go and have a look then," the policeman said dubiously.

"You may want to drive, sir, as it's rather a long way," Phil suggested. "Maybe I could come with you and the others could ride?"

They were about to follow through with this idea when Emily spotted Mrs. Baker walking up the driveway.

"Mother!" Phil said in surprise. "How did you get here?"

"I walked," Mrs. Baker answered. "Hello," she said to the police officers, anxiety in her voice. "Can I come along?"

They quickly agreed, and Mrs. Baker and Phil were soon sitting in the back of the car, Phil directing the policemen where to go. From his perspective in the car watching the others riding along, he could see why their story seemed difficult to believe.

When they arrived at the hill they had left in a rush, Andy suddenly gasped and leaped off Sergeant's back, racing over to the tripod. "I left the camera running!" he cried.

"There goes the battery," Seth replied.

"No, that's not what I mean! I've probably recorded the whole performance!"

He rushed over to the police car, explaining what had happened and playing the footage for the men to see. He felt color rising to his cheeks as the police watched the final scene of their film, and was relieved to see Phil finally drop down low to peer over the hill. All the children ran up the hill, and then Geronimo approached the camera. Next thing, the footage was a blur, there was a thud, and then they could see the clear, blue sky.

"I guess that's it," Andy said, about to stop playback.

"No, wait," Phil instructed. "We might catch a glimpse of that helicopter!"

They waited and waited for what seemed a very long time, when eventually there was a whirring noise growing ever louder and a smudge on the screen as the helicopter passed.

"There it is!" Andy cried. "I can't believe it!"

"Thank the Lord!" Mrs. Baker sighed in relief.

The policemen were impressed at the footage. "Well done for thinking of that," one of them said. "Now show us where the chopper landed."

They continued on, driving around the hill and straight to the spot they had been ten minutes before. The men got out of the car and requested that the children stay out of the circle they were examining so as not to damage any footprints in the loosened soil.

"Could you describe any of the men you saw?" the other asked.

Phil shook his head. "They were too far away."

"And the chopper?"

"That was white. I'm afraid I was too shocked and distracted by the men to notice any more."

"What did the men appear to be doing?"

Phil thought for a moment as he tried to replay the scene in his mind. "Bending over, pulling, pushing, lifting—in general, they were just busy."

"That sounds very suspicious," Mrs. Baker said. "Do you think they may have been planting something on the property?"

"It's possible," Phil said, "but they would have had to bury it and cover it over. I don't think they would risk leaving something here once they knew they had been seen."

"Exactly," the policeman said. "Even so, I'm going to request permission to dig up this ground. We may find clues if nothing else."

****

"Father!" Abby gasped as she heard the car pull to a stop.

"Let's go and ask what he saw!" Andy exclaimed, sprinting toward the house.

The children had all come back to the Baker home once the police left, and had changed out of their costumes and eaten a snack. They had been playing a game out in the garden when the sound of tires on the driveway had alerted them to Mr. Baker's arrival.

They all ran around the house, meeting Mr. Baker as he walked up to the front door.

"Hello Father; what did you see?" Andy asked immediately.

Mr. Baker frowned. "I waited in my car in a distant parking space with a good view of that tree. Three o'clock came and went, and there was nobody to be seen."

Just then the front door opened, and Mrs. Baker and Phil came out to hear the conversation.

"Nothing happened," Mr. Baker said to them.

"Do you think the person the note was meant for had been warned not to come?" Abby thought aloud.

"It's possible," Mr. Baker said, "but I was very discreet. I began to wonder if the whole thing wasn't just a ruse."

"A ruse?" both Tom and Laura asked.

"A trick," Mr. Baker said.

"Of course it was!" Phil exclaimed suddenly, snapping his fingers. "Mr. Larone knew we would be tricked by his note and would all head to the tree this afternoon. He must have also known that Mr. and Mrs. Wilbur were going out. With all of us accounted for, it was the perfect opportunity to do something illegal on Mr. Wilbur's farm."

"Mr. Larone?" Mrs. Baker gasped. "Do you think he was behind that?"

"Behind what? What are you talking about?" Mr. Baker asked. Nobody had yet told him of the events at the Wilbur farm that afternoon.

Phil quickly plunged into the story. "We didn't want to call you in case you were in a dangerous position requiring silence," he finished.

Mr. Baker's face was a picture of surprise and disbelief. "I can't believe we were so easily deceived! Has anybody told Jed and Hannah?"

Mrs. Baker nodded. "I called them as soon as we got back here. They were very shocked, as you can imagine, and are only too eager for the police to go ahead and investigate."

"What if those men in the helicopter come back? They might not have finished what they were doing," Emily said thoughtfully.

101

Mrs. Baker gasped at the idea.

"They'll know how dangerous such an action would be, but might be desperate enough to try it," Mr. Baker said. "If the police aren't going to keep watch overnight, I'll suggest to Jed that he and I do it. Hannah and the children could spend the night here, as an extra precaution."

That evening, the plan was followed through. The Wilburs were grateful for the Bakers' offer, and Mrs. Wilbur and the children prepared for a night away from home, while the two men and Phil got things ready for an overnight watch in the fields.

Before darkness fell, the fathers decided on a sheltered position on the border of a field as their lookout, and then they and Phil set out their sleeping bags.

"I doubt we'll see anything tonight," Phil said, "not when those crooks know we'll be at our most watchful."

Mr. Wilbur nodded. "Still, it's better to be safe than sorry. I can't imagine what they were doing on my land."

"Neither can I," Mr. Baker agreed. "The police said they hadn't found anything yet, right?"

"Right," Mr. Wilbur replied. "They've dug up the disturbed area to a depth of almost three feet already, and not found a single thing. They'd like to continue tomorrow, but don't expect their results to be any different."

Phil frowned. "If they don't seem to be burying anything on your land, it follows that they must have been digging something up."

"But what?" Mr. Wilbur sighed in thought.

They continued talking quietly as the sky darkened, and then they ate their packed supper and drank hot coffee from their large flasks. As time wore on, they decided to each take three-hour shifts all through the night, listening for an engine or any signs of activity. Mr. Wilbur volunteered to take the first shift, and soon the field was quiet as Mr. Baker and Phil settled down to sleep until they were awakened for their turns.

Back at the Baker house, the excited younger children had a hard time settling down, and viewed the scenario as something they should do more often. Emily and Laura were staying in Abby's room, and Seth, John, and Tom had set up camp in Andy's room. Mrs. Wilbur and Zachary were going to stay in the spare room. The girls lay on their beds and stayed awake, chatting about the mystery.

"Have you ever wondered whose story is right—Mr. Larone's or Mr. James's?" Emily asked.

"Many times," Abby said.

"They both would've heard the story from their parents, who were told the story by their parents, and so on. Neither Mr. Larone nor Mr. James would know for sure that their story was accurate, only that they have retold it just the way they heard it," Emily said.

"I know, and that makes it almost impossible for us to judge between them without knowing the facts ourselves," Abby replied. "It's easier to believe Mr. James because his character is more trustworthy than Mr. Larone's."

"Yes, but that's no proof his ancestors told the story honestly. I found Mr. James's story interesting because it had a lot to do with Haggai—you know, the guy who reportedly stole the ring from Victor and then became an outlaw. I've been thinking a lot, and I don't think it was his fault he became a criminal, if he did, that is. He had such a rough upbringing with a lazy, drunken dad, without a mom to love him, that his adult life is quite understandable."

Abby raised herself onto her elbow and looked at her friend with a frown. Her heart was trembling but her voice was steady as she asked, "Are you serious?"

"Yes," Emily replied, looking equally surprised. "You don't agree?"

Abby took a deep breath and began slowly. "Not if you mean what I think you do. None of us have perfect parents, and while I will concede that some upbringings are harder than others, we are still responsible for our lives—the decisions we make, the thoughts we think, and the character we build. Haggai had a hard time, but—but there are plenty of biblical examples of people who rose above their circumstances by not allowing themselves to become bitter."

"Biblical examples? Like who?"

"Look at Joseph, who was sold into slavery by his own brothers when he was a young man. Talk about sibling rivalry! He was later put into prison for something he didn't do, and ultimately had to endure all those trials for many years—and he came out of it an upright, humble man.

All I'm saying is that Haggai's father was responsible for his own actions, just as Haggai was responsible for Haggai's actions, just as Emily is responsible for Emily's actions, just as I'm responsible for mine."

"Okay, okay." Emily laughed. "I get it. But I still feel sorry for Haggai."

The next morning, just after breakfast, the men came back from their night vigil and were welcomed warmly.

"Nothing happened," Mr. Wilbur said in answer to the questions all around, "but I'm glad we can be sure those men didn't come back."

The Wilburs packed up their belongings and carried them to the car before thanking the Bakers for their help and hospitality.

"You two look exhausted," Mrs. Baker said sympathetically once the Wilburs had left. "Was it hard to sleep last night?"

"Camping out in the open always takes a bit of adjusting to," Mr. Baker said.

Phil nodded, stifling a yawn. "The air was cold, too, and the ground was really hard."

"Ooh, Phil," Andy teased, "you're not going soft, are you? Is luxury finding its way into your old bones?"

Mr. Baker laughed. "I think we'd better arrange a proper camping trip sometime so Andy doesn't have to miss out."

"That's a great idea," Mrs. Baker said as the others chuckled.

"For now, though," Mr. Baker said, "I think it's time you children thought about schoolwork again."

The children tried their best to put aside the distractions of the last few days and concentrate on their work, a task they all found nearly impossible. At lunchtime, to their surprise, Mr. Baker announced that he had just heard some disturbing news.

"What is it?" Tom asked.

"Mr. Larone was in a car accident."

CHAPTER 11

"Is he hurt?" Mrs. Baker asked immediately.

"He was concussed, and was sent straight to the hospital."

"Concussed? What's that?" Tom asked.

"Mr. Larone was knocked unconscious because of a blow to the head," Mr. Baker replied. "The doctor thinks he'll be all right." He frowned. "But what really caught my attention is this: as he slowly came around, Mr. Larone was said to have been muttering a rhyme, over and over again."

The others waited tensely, hoping their father had been told what the rhyme was.

"One of the nurses wrote it down. Listen:

"'Two hundred fathoms *east*,

An excavator's feast.

Two hundred fathoms west,

You will find the rest.'

"I've been trying to figure out what it possibly could mean," Mr. Baker finished.

"Fathoms," Phil muttered with a frown. "That's a unit for measuring the depth of water, isn't it?"

Mr. Baker nodded. "One fathom is the equivalent of six feet."

"But why talk about measuring the depth of water and then refer to excavation in the very next line?" Abby wondered aloud.

"That's what I don't get," Mr. Baker answered. "Another thing I can't understand is the reference to 'Two hundred fathoms east.' The only way to measure depth is to go *down*, not east or west."

"Well, that's a riddle to keep us busy for awhile," Andy said. "I can't imagine us solving that one in a hurry."

"Who told you all this?" Mrs. Baker asked, changing the subject.

"Jed," Mr. Baker replied. "Apparently Hannah is friends with one of the nurses who tended to Mr. Larone. She told Hannah everything, including the interesting information that when Mr. Larone finally regained full consciousness, he vehemently denied any knowledge of the riddle."

Mrs. Baker frowned. "That's strange. Either it's buried so deep in his memory that he can't remember it, or he doesn't want anybody to know about it."

"Exactly."

"I wonder if the riddle has anything to do with the men and the helicopter," Phil said. "If they've only fulfilled the first part of it, they might go back to Mr. Wilbur's farm."

"Are you suggesting another night watch?" Mr. Baker queried a little reluctantly.

"Not exactly. If that's the case, though, we need to figure out what the riddle means before they come back."

"Good point," Abby said.

"What about the police?" Andy asked. "Have they continued digging in Mr. Wilbur's field?"

"Yes, they finished their investigation about an hour ago. I don't think they found anything at all."

They all sat in the living room after their meal, trying to look at the riddle from different angles and tease out its meaning.

"Here's the riddle again," Mr. Baker said.

"'Two hundred fathoms east,

An excavator's feast.

Two hundred fathoms west,

You will find the rest.'"

"The rest . . . the rest of what?" Abby thought aloud.

"The rest of whatever you found the first time," Andy said.

"Yes," Phil said, "and the first time, you found an excavator's feast."

"What exactly is an excavator, Father?" Tom asked.

"Well, to *excavate* is to dig up soil or archeological finds, so an *excavator* would be a person who engages in such activities."

"Those men in Mr. Wilbur's field really looked like excavators," Andy muttered with a frown.

"They did," Phil agreed.

"If they really were excavating," Abby began, "they were following the directions of the first half of the riddle. But to follow the second half, they would have to go somewhere else."

"Exactly!" Mr. Baker exclaimed, snapping his fingers. "We assumed they would come back to the same spot, but if this riddle really is what they were following, they would go somewhere different the second time."

"Which is why we need to know where they'll be going, so they can be caught," Mrs. Baker put in.

"How do we figure out where they'll go?" Tom asked.

"To do that, we need to find out how they followed the first set of directions: 'two hundred fathoms east.'" Mr. Baker rubbed his brow in thought. "Phil, please pass the map."

Phil pulled a map of the surrounding area from a drawer and handed it to his father, who spread it out on the low table for all to see.

"Do you think the men might have dug a hole two hundred fathoms deep, and found the hidden object on the east side of the hole?" Abby suggested.

"If they did that, they'd be mining," Andy said, stifling a chuckle.

"Two hundred fathoms is twelve hundred feet, which is almost a quarter of a mile," Phil said slowly as he calculated. "They'd have to have pretty amazing equipment to dig that far that fast, Abs," he finished, trying to be more tactful than Andy.

"All right, all right." Abby blushed. "What about the water aspect, then? You said fathoms measure the depth of water."

"Maybe that's a side issue," Mr. Baker said. "Maybe the main thing to focus on is that fathoms measure depth. In that case, the riddle might direct a person to travel two hundred fathoms east and then—dig."

Phil frowned. "Two hundred fathoms is almost a quarter of a mile . . ."

"You'd need a starting place," Andy said.

"How are we going to figure out what that is?" Abby sighed. "This is beginning to sound hopeless."

"Not quite," Mr. Baker replied with a shake of his head. "Phil, we camped about here, didn't we?"

Phil leaned over to see the place on the map his father was pointing to. "Yes, that's right. The helicopter was somewhere around here." He placed his finger a little away from his father's.

"Okay. If we're right, the men traveled two hundred fathoms east to get to this spot," Mr. Baker continued, "so to find their starting point, we need to move a quarter mile west."

"What a genius idea!" Abby gasped as they all leaned forward to watch.

Referring to the map's key, Mr. Baker measured out the distance of a quarter mile and studied the area where his approximation landed. "This is still the Wilburs' property, isn't it?"

"I think so," Andy said after a moment's reflection.

"Yes, yes it is," Phil confirmed. Then he gasped. "If I'm right, this spot is the location of the old stables where we found the ring!"

The others looked incredulous as they tried to take it in.

"So the two incidences are related, after all!" Abby cried.

"Of course," Mr. Baker said slowly, shaking his head in realization. "So if those men come back, they'll head a quarter mile west of the old stables."

"We need to phone Jed and let him know," Mrs. Baker said.

"If we're not already too late." Mr. Baker jumped up to grab the telephone.

The Bakers hurriedly piled into their car once Mr. Baker was off the phone and drove straight to the Wilburs' farmhouse.

"We'd better hurry up and see if your deductions are right," Mr. Wilbur said as he came out the house, followed by his oldest children.

"I think I'll stay with Hannah," Mrs. Baker said quickly.

Mr. Baker nodded. He mentally counted the number of children eager to come along, and realized they'd need to take both vehicles.

The Wilburs climbed into their car.

"Follow me," Mr. Wilbur said.

Mr. Baker swung his car off the driveway to follow the Wilburs as they drove straight for the old stables. The trip seemed to take a long time because of the urgency everybody felt. The opening and closing of gates and the bumpy ride all made the experience feel laboriously slow.

Finally, when they got to the site of the old stables, they all tumbled out of the cars. Mr. Wilbur grabbed a measuring wheel and a compass from the trunk and strode forward, starting his measurement above the old cellar.

"West," he muttered, waiting for the compass to stabilize and then rolling the measuring wheel in a straight line. They all walked beside him, feeling they were doing their bit as they watched. He kept glancing from the compass to the digital screen of the device to make sure his measurement was accurate.

They continued in this way for several minutes, until Mr. Wilbur announced, "This is just under a quarter of a mile west of the old stables."

They stopped and surveyed the area critically. At a glance, they could see nothing unusual, so they began examining the ground, looking out for any sorts of landmarks. The dark, rich soil was scattered with weeds except for a small area that was clear of them.

"Emily," Abby said suddenly, "remember that time we were out riding and we saw those tire tracks?"

"Yes," Emily replied, realization beginning to show on her face.

"Those must have belonged to a car those men drove!"

"Tire tracks?" Mr. Baker asked, immediately alert. "Where did you see them?"

The girls thought hard. "We were near here, actually," Emily answered. "I can't remember the exact route we took."

Just then, Tom, who was peering up at the sky, let out a cry. "Look!" He pointed anxiously. "Look, up there!"

The others followed his terrified gaze to see a helicopter in the distance. The sound of the whirling blades was growing louder every second.

CHAPTER 12

Both of the fathers reached for their phones immediately, the same thought on their minds.

"The police!"

Mr. Baker canceled his call as Mr. Wilbur was connected, and looked up at the approaching chopper.

"Take cover!" he commanded the children, who were panicking. "Come and huddle around these trees!"

The helicopter hovered just overhead, and for a few sickening moments Mr. Baker wondered if the crooked men would take them all captive. The craft lowered, paused as if undecided, and then slowly rose into the air again. A grim face was staring angrily down from the window, until it was lost from sight.

Tom was clinging tightly to his father, whimpering in fear, and the others found themselves speechless and gasping to get their breath back.

"Thank the Lord," Mr. Baker muttered, flooded with relief. He looked around at the children, all safe, who were thinking the same thing. "That was close."

"It's a shame we couldn't catch them," Mr. Wilbur said, "but I'm grateful to the Lord for protecting the children."

"Absolutely. Now we know this is the right place, we can begin searching for whatever it is they were after," Mr. Baker said.

The police arrived in a few minutes, and the whole scenario was explained. Then the girls were asked to show where they had seen the tire tracks. Slightly flustered by the weight of the responsibility, they found it hard to remember where they had ridden. Working together, they retraced the route they had taken on horseback, and finally stopped and pointed.

"There they are!" Abby exclaimed. "Those are the ones we saw."

The policemen examined the tracks and took photographs of them, with Andy snapping shots too.

When the police had left, the fathers and children drove straight back to the Wilbur farmhouse. Some told the mothers what had happened, while the rest grabbed all the digging implements they could find and packed them into the cars.

They hurried back to the spot they'd just left, itching with anticipation.

"The measurement led us here," Mr. Wilbur announced, plunging a spade into the ground. His face immediately took on a surprised expression. "Why, this ground is soft!"

They all began digging with gusto, finding his statement to be true.

"It must have been recently disturbed," Mr. Baker said.

"Those men must have been digging here. Don't tell me they have completed their business already," Seth muttered.

"Well, they were coming back for something," Andy pointed out. "We must try to find out what it is."

They all worked steadily, the hole growing bit by bit, until Emily cried out, "Hey, what's that?"

Following her gaze and pointed finger, the others could make out something half-buried in the soil. Mr. Wilbur stepped forward and scooped it up in his spade, placing it on the ground beside the hole.

"It looks like . . . like . . ." Seth's voice trailed off.

"What is it?" John asked, leaning forward for a better view.

"This looks like a piece of rough leather or other sturdy material. My guess would be that it's come off a heavy gardening glove, perfect for this sort of work." Mr. Wilbur motioned to the hole they were digging. "Let's continue, keeping our eyes peeled for any other objects like that."

They worked for a solid half-hour, at which point the girls sat down, almost too tired to talk. John and Tom, who had stopped earlier, were playing nearby. Andy and Seth were trying to last as long as they could, but even they had to admit they were exhausted.

"I think we should be heading home soon," Mr. Baker eventually said, glancing at his watch. "It's after five o'clock."

Mr. Wilbur straightened up. "Yes. All of you have done a great job."

The boys flopped on the ground, and Phil sat down beside them, rubbing his aching shoulder. "I can't believe we're too late every time," he said. "First, we think we're on to something when we spot men in the other field. The police dig a deep hole and don't find anything. Now this."

"It's déjà vu," Andy muttered, glad to use a little of the French he'd learned.

"The tragedy is that there were only two locations mentioned in the clue," Abby said, cupping her chin in her hand, "and we've missed both of them."

"What were those guys coming back for, anyway?" Emily added.

"The only thing I can think of is that they came back to erase those tire tracks," Mr. Baker said.

Mr. Wilbur's eyebrows shot up. "Oh, now that's a good guess."

They returned to the house feeling very tired and deflated. Mr. Wilbur thanked the Bakers for all they had done that day, after which the Bakers drove home. The evening chores seemed to take forever, and by the time supper and family devotions were complete, everybody was ready for bed.

The Bakers all got up early the next morning, refreshed by their good night's sleep. At breakfast, Mr. Baker said he would call Mr. Larone to find out how he was recovering after his accident.

The old man was as curt and snappy in his remarks as he had ever been, and Mr. Baker arrived at the conclusion that he was not badly hurt, though his car was a write-off.

"Well, that's that," Mr. Baker said to the others as he hung up. "Mr. Larone seems all right. He made the accident seem like the other person's fault, though I heard quite a different story from Jed. He was told that Mr. Larone caused the crash by speeding."

"Maybe we should go and investigate the scene of the accident," Phil suggested.

"Yes," Andy agreed.

"Where was Mr. Larone going in such a hurry?" Abby wondered aloud.

"We can only guess," Mr. Baker replied. "We did find out the location of the crash, so I suppose having a look around would do no harm."

They set out soon afterward.

"How long are we going to drive?" Tom asked.

"For about twenty minutes," Mr. Baker answered. "Mr. Larone was heading north and was about to join the freeway when the collision happened."

Andy sighed. "I wish there was some way we could find out where he was heading."

"There might have been a way," Phil said.

"What is it?" Abby asked immediately.

"Well, if he was using a GPS, the location would automatically be saved under 'Recent Destinations,'" Phil said. "However, the GPS could have been smashed in the wreck."

"That's a good point, Phil," Abby praised. She became thoughtful. "I wonder if there's a way we or the police could get our hands on his device if it wasn't damaged."

"You're both assuming he was using a GPS device in the first place," Andy hastily pointed out. "He might not have been."

Mr. Baker found a place to pull up near the spot he'd been told the wreck had happened. The road was relatively quiet at that time of the mid-morning, and since it was not the freeway, the Bakers got out to investigate.

"This is the corner Mr. Larone turned without first checking for traffic," Mr. Baker said, re-enacting the accident on foot. "A lady was already driving along this road, and when Mr. Larone turned without warning, she couldn't brake in time and there was a big collision. Mr. Larone's car came way up the curb here."

He crossed the road, pointing out skid marks along the road, leading to where black marks streaked the sidewalk. They spent some time walking out the scenario and following the skid marks, and they were about to leave when Andy let out a gasp.

"Look here!" he exclaimed, squatting on the sidewalk and peering at the nearby grass. He pointed and motioned frantically, encouraging the others to hurry over and see the cause of his excited behavior. They gathered around him.

"Look here!" he repeated. "Father, you said Mr. Larone's car was pushed all the way up the curb. Well, right here it seems his car went a little further than the sidewalk, because there are tire tread-marks in the mud, between the blades of grass." The others slowly realized what statement he might make next. "I'm sure these are the same tires that made the tread-marks in Mr. Wilbur's field!"

Abby's eyebrows shot up. "Of course! We already think Mr. Larone is involved in the strange activity on Mr. Wilbur's farm, and this could be great evidence!"

"Wait a minute," Mr. Baker cautioned. "Andy, can you prove the tread-marks are exactly the same?"

Andy nodded vigorously, removing his camera from around his neck. "Last night when the police took photos of the tire tracks, I did too." He paused a moment. "Here they are."

Mr. Baker took the camera from his son's outstretched hands and studied the photo before kneeling down to examine the hardened track beside the sidewalk. "Yes," he finally muttered, "yes, they do seem to correspond."

"Well done, Andy," Mrs. Baker praised.

A tinge of smugness came over his face, and he shrugged. "It was easy."

"You'd better take a picture of these tracks too," Mr. Baker directed, handing the camera back.

"What do we do now?" Phil asked. "We feel sure Mr. Larone has some part in the mystery, but have no way to prove it for sure."

"We just have to keep on looking," Mr. Baker replied, "and pray for a way to figure out what's going on."

CHAPTER 13

They were on their way home when Mrs. Baker said, "I need to pop into the store quickly—we're running low on bread and milk and Abby and I forgot about them last time we went."

They altered their course slightly, and when the car pulled into the store's parking lot, Mrs. Baker and Abby jumped out.

They entered the store and walked briskly down the aisles. On passing a rack of clothes with a large "sale" sign on it, Mrs. Baker paused. "This is a nice sweater for your father. Abby, please run along and get the items while I look for his size."

Abby did as she was told, returning to the rack a few minutes later where her mother was turning away empty-handed.

"None of them will fit," Mrs. Baker explained, "not even Andy. The only size left is extra large."

"There's not even a single medium left? That's a shame." Abby frowned, trying to remember something. "Medium—why does that ring a bell?" she muttered to herself.

When the ladies got back to the car, Abby clambered inside and immediately turned to Andy. "Medium—does that sound familiar at all?"

Andy frowned. "Er . . . yes. What do you mean?"

"Of course!" she exclaimed suddenly. "Now I remember! When Mr. Wilbur told us about the inscription on the back of the ring, I'm completely sure one of the words he used was 'medium.'"

"Oh-h." Andy nodded. "Now I understand. It was a Latin phrase like 'medium soap' or 'sud medium.' Why do you want to know?"

"I'm sure it's important," Abby replied. "Whatever it was, it meant something like 'under half.'"

"How could that help?" Phil asked, his face blank.

"I remember the inscription," Mr. Baker said. "Jed told me it was '*supter in medius*,' which basically translates into 'below the middle.'"

"'Below the middle,'" Abby repeated. "Why go to the trouble of inscribing that on a ring? It's got to be something meaningful."

"Maybe there was some secret that could be discovered beneath the middle of the ruby," Andy suggested.

"Mr. Larone knew of the inscription," Phil thought aloud, "but said he didn't know what it meant."

They were pulling out of the parking space when Mr. Baker said, "Why don't we pay Mr. Larone a visit? There's a secret here that somebody doesn't want us to know about, and I'm sure he could give us a clue as to what that is, whether he means to or not."

Consequently, in fifteen minutes' time the Baker car pulled up outside Mr. Larone's house, and Mr. Baker rang the doorbell. The door was opened a few minutes later by a surprised Bud Larone.

"Hello. Can I help you?" he asked.

"Hello, Bud," Mr. Baker replied pleasantly. "We've just come from the scene of your accident. How are you feeling?"

"From what we could see, the crash must have been pretty serious," Phil added.

"I'm just as fine as I was this morning."

The Bakers couldn't think of anything to say until Tom piped up with, "Mother, I need to use the bathroom."

"Can't you wait until we get home, dear?" Mrs. Baker asked, trying to avert the awkwardness it would cause.

Tom shook his head. "I need it *really badly.*"

Mrs. Baker looked up at Mr. Larone. "Uh, could Tom please—"

"Go on," Mr. Larone interrupted. "Down the passage, second door to the right. I suppose the rest of you will have to come in."

"Thank you so much," Mrs. Baker said as she stepped inside to help Tom find the bathroom.

The others followed Mr. Larone into the living room, where he offered for them to sit down. Having not much else to do, the twins glanced around the room at the old piano, the grubby window, and the shelf with antique ornaments on it.

"Do you like antiques?" Abby asked, hoping to break the tense silence.

"I got them from my grandfather."

Abby frowned, her mind wandering back to something Mr. Davis had said. "Is he the one who liked archeology?"

Mr. Larone's eyes flashed suddenly. "What's it to you?"

"Oh, I was . . . just asking," she stammered.

Mrs. Baker soon joined them. "We heard your car was written off," she began sympathetically. "Hopefully you'll be able to acquire another one or make a plan with relatives. It must be very hard to get around otherwise."

"I don't need to get around," Mr. Larone replied coldly.

"Well, I'm sure you'll need groceries eventually," Mrs. Baker countered. She glanced at her husband. "We could offer to help you from time to time, if necessary."

Mr. Baker nodded.

"I don't need help."

Mrs. Baker pressed her lips into a thin line, struggling to think of a self-controlled reply.

"Well, if it so happens that there are errands you need to run," Mr. Baker continued, "perhaps we can come up with something. Is there anything you can think of, off the top of your head, that you needed to do in the last few days?"

Mr. Larone thought for a moment, then shook his head.

"What about the day of your accident—did you need to do anything important?" Mr. Baker asked.

That question was evidently too sharp, because Mr. Larone's eyes narrowed in suspicion and his mouth set in a grim curve. "No," he growled. "I've told you already—I don't need to run any errands, I don't need to get around, and I don't need help! Now if there's nothing else you want to know, I suggest you go some place where your charity will be appreciated!"

With that, he rose to his feet and led the way to the front door, holding it open as the Bakers filed out. Then the door closed with a firm shove, and the Bakers made their way back to the car, their minds whirling.

"That didn't go so well," Andy stated dryly. "Maybe he thought we weren't being helpful enough."

Abby attempted a smile, but her voice was sad. "Some people can't recognize kindness when they see it."

"Partly so," Mr. Baker agreed, "but remember, we were going there to gather information. Mr. Larone must have sensed it. After all, I was hoping to find out where he was heading at the time of his accident."

They had driven around the corner when suddenly Mrs. Baker let out a gasp. "Tom!" she cried, staring aghast at her husband. "We forgot about Tom!"

CHAPTER 14

Tom pulled the chain and went over to the basin, humming softly. He rubbed his hands with soap until a thick, creamy lather covered them, and then he worked the substance all over the backs of his hands until they were completely white.

"Oh no, I have leprosy!" he whispered in a make-believe voice. "What must I do?"

He changed his whisper to a higher, girl's pitch. "You must go and see Elisha, Lord Naaman."

Back came the deeper whisper, "Elisha, what must I do?"

Then, in an even hoarser whisper, came the reply. "Naaman, you must wash in the river Jordan."

Then Tom turned on the faucet and pretended to laugh quietly with joy as the water washed the soap away. "It worked!" he whispered, still in his make-believe voice. "I am clean!"

Humming again, he dried his hands, opened the door, and went down the passage. To his surprise, the living room was empty. Scared, he went back into the hall where he could hear Mr. Larone's voice. Following the sound of the voice, he came to the study, where the elderly man was on the phone. Tom had waited patiently for a few moments before Mr. Larone noticed him there. The man's face showed plain shock and surprise at the sight of the boy, and he immediately set down the phone.

"Get out!" he bellowed. "Get out, now!"

Tom backed out of the study, his blue eyes wide as saucers. *Have I done something wrong?* he wondered, retreating as fast as the fearsome man approached. *I knew it wouldn't have been polite to interrupt, so why . . . ?*

"What are you doing here?" Mr. Larone yelled.

"I—used the—the bathroom," Tom muttered, his lip beginning to quiver.

"The bathroom? The bathroom! That's a lie! What did you hear?"

Tom shrunk back against the wall, his small body trembling.

"I asked, 'What did you hear?' Answer me!"

"I . . . I . . ."

Suddenly, there was a loud banging on the front door, and Tom flinched in fright.

"That'll be your troublesome parents!" Mr. Larone exclaimed as he hurried forward.

Mr. Baker was on the doorstep, his face anxious, and he let out a breath when Tom raced out and clung to him.

"Take your little eavesdropper with you this time!" Mr. Larone shouted. "And don't come back!"

"There's no need to be so angry," Mr. Baker returned indignantly, but the front door had already slammed. Turning, he scooped up his son and walked back to the car.

"You poor dear!" Mrs. Baker said as she saw her little boy on the verge of tears and unable to speak.

"What happened?" Mr. Baker asked, sitting in the driver's seat and propping Tom on his lap.

Tom took a few breaths and then told the story, trying bravely to hold back spilling teardrops.

"Poor you," Abby said sympathetically. "*I'd* be scared of Mr. Larone by myself."

"What did you overhear of the phone conversation?" Mr. Baker asked, changing the subject.

"Nothing much," Tom replied, "at least, nothing important."

"Just tell us what you heard."

"Well, Mr. Larone only mentioned something about the last crate and clearing everything up afterward," Tom said, straining to remember.

"The last crate?" Mr. Baker repeated, his eyes wide.

Tom nodded.

"Crate of what?" Mrs. Baker wondered aloud.

"This just might have something to do with the strange goings-on at the Wilburs' farm," Mr. Baker breathed in disbelief.

"Why?" the twins asked in unison.

"The ring was found in a crate on the Wilburs' farm," Mr. Baker began. "What if those two strange events on the farm were to do with *other* crates? After all, Mr. Larone said 'the *last* crate.'"

"If it is, we need to get over there quickly and figure out where it might be hidden," Phil said urgently.

"Yes!" Mr. Baker agreed. He gave Tom's shoulder a reassuring squeeze. "Tom, get into your seat. This is a matter of utmost importance." His face became grim. "Mr. Larone mentioned eavesdropping, so he knows you heard something. He's going to be sure to tell his friends to hurry up and leave us with a baffling riddle we'll never solve."

They rushed to their friends' farm and were ushered into the house by a surprised Mrs. Wilbur.

"Is Jed home?" Mr. Baker asked quickly.

"Yes, he's in his study," Mrs. Wilbur replied.

"Good—I need a word with him right away!"

Mr. Wilbur must have heard the commotion, because he soon appeared at the top of the stairs and descended hurriedly.

"Hi, everybody—what's going on?"

"We have good reason to think those men and the helicopter will come back very soon for the last time." Mr. Baker then told the story in a minute or two.

The Wilburs, who had been joined by most of their children, looked concerned and flustered.

"How do we know where they'll strike this time?" Mrs. Wilbur moaned.

"That's what we have to figure out," Mr. Wilbur said decisively. "What about that riddle we followed last time? Could there be a cryptic clue in there somewhere?"

"Cryp-tic?" Tom repeated.

"A message with a hidden meaning," Mr. Baker briefly explained. "Can one of you kids remember the riddle? I don't think I'd recall all of it."

"'Two hundred fathoms east, an excavator's feast. Two hundred fathoms west, you will find the rest,'" Abby recited.

"A code, perhaps?" Mr. Wilbur said. "Well, I'm pretty sure the men won't be going back to either of the spots we and the police excavated, because there definitely weren't any crates left there."

Nobody seemed able to think of anything, until Phil said, "Then what about the inscription on the back of the ring? That seems to be the only clue-like thing we're left with."

"*Supter in medius*—beneath the middle?" Mr. Wilbur questioned. He nodded slowly. "Yes, that does sound like a clue."

"Beneath the middle—the middle of what?" Mr. Baker wondered aloud.

"The middle of the farm?" Andy suggested. Then he shook his head. "No. I guess the borders of the property would've changed over the years. We'll never work out where to look in time."

"The middle of the house, maybe?" Seth said. "Nah, I guess not."

"I think it's the middle of the ring, as Andy earlier suggested," Abby said. "There could be another clue beneath the ruby."

"No," Mr. Wilbur disagreed, "I think I would've noticed something like that."

"The reference would have to be something stable," Phil said, "something unchangeable by time."

"Stable," Mr. Baker repeated, catching on to that word. "Stable. That's it! That must be the place!"

"What do you mean? Where? How?" Everybody wanted to know.

"I know it sounds crazy, but I think the last crate is buried beneath the old stables."

"The ones we pulled down?" Mr. Wilbur asked.

"Yes. Remember, we found a cellar and some crates beneath them," Mr. Baker said.

"Do you mean we've already found the last crate?" Mrs. Wilbur asked. "The one with the ring in it?"

Mr. Baker hesitated. "No, we couldn't have found the last one. You see, we had to find those crates to find the ring, which held the clue to the last crate. The last crate would be impossible to locate if the clue to finding it was hidden inside. I think we ought to look *under the cellar.*"

"I still don't understand why you think that's the right spot," Mr. Wilbur said with a frown.

"Think of the riddle: 'two hundred fathoms east, and two hundred fathoms west.' Combining those directions makes a line four hundred fathoms long. What's the '*supter in medius*' of that?"

"'*Supter in medius*' is beneath the middle," Mr. Wilbur said, calculating, "and the middle of the four-hundred fathom line is . . . the old stables." His eyebrows shot up. "We'd better head over there right away!"

They rushed to the cars, bringing some tools with them from the garage.

"Hannah," Mr. Wilbur said, "could you please stay here in case we need you to bring more tools?"

"Oh, yes, I'm going to stay here with Laura and Zac," Mrs. Wilbur said, "and I'll prepare lunch for when you get back."

"I'll stay with Tom," Mrs. Baker said.

The others hopped in the two cars, Mr. Wilbur leading the bumpy way to the north field.

"Here it is," Mr. Wilbur said, leaping out. There were eight "bangs" as eight car-doors were hurriedly shut, and the children gathered, breathless, around the site of the old stables. The fathers wasted no time in swinging open the cellar door, and they all peered into the cavity beneath.

"Last time we opened the cellar it was dusk," Andy observed. "I remember we used my flashlight to check that nothing was left in here."

"And we could have missed something," Phil added.

"So what are we going to do?" Seth asked. "We don't exactly have time to dig the cellar away."

"No," Mr. Baker replied, "but we might be able to remove this stone slab constituting the floor."

Mr. Baker grabbed a spade and shoved it around the edges of the stone, then tried to lever it upwards. Mr. Wilbur grabbed another spade to help.

"It's looser than one would expect," Mr. Baker puffed. "It can't have been sealed in place at all."

With a sudden scraping sound, the stone loosened further. The men doubled their efforts, trying to lift it out of the cellar. It was very heavy, and Phil and the boys soon found a way to help, slipping a rope under the stone and using it to pull from the other side.

"It's almost up," Abby encouraged. "Just a little way to go now."

The fathers no longer needed their spades for leverage, instead using their hands to push the slab vertical.

"Whew! Well, we got it upright," said Seth, who had been helping to pull on the rope.

They crowded around to see what was under the slab, but all that was visible was hard-packed earth. Working together, they heaved the slab out of the hole.

"What do we do now?" Seth asked.

"Now we dig," Mr. Wilbur answered, grabbing his spade.

The fathers plunged their tools into the earth, loosening the soil until their spades struck something hard. They were breathing deeply and their faces were flushed as they stepped back to evaluate the situation. The boys were only too eager to continue the work, so the fathers watched as they uncovered a layer of wood.

"It looks like a crate," Phil said, panting. "How are we going to get it out? The soil is hard-packed all around it."

"Why bother? Let's just lift the lid and see what's beneath," Seth suggested.

The fathers decided to follow up on that idea, knowing that they were pressed for time.

"Let's at least find out what those crooks have been after," Mr. Wilbur said.

They pried around the wood to make a little space, and then began levering it up with the spades. The work was tough, and the men paused to catch their breath several times. Finally, they and the boys managed to peel the lid back with a heave and it came off with a final groan.

"Ouch! Splinter!" Seth cried, examining his finger, but the others paid no attention. They were all staring down into the crate.

It was full of sawdust, which Mr. Wilbur shoved away with one hand, revealing a few strangely shaped objects wrapped in brown paper. He reached out to grasp one, holding it gently in his hands as he unwrapped it. All eyes were riveted as he peeled back layer after layer of paper. Hearts thumped. Breaths were held. Fingers tingled with curiosity. *Will we finally discover the cause for all the . . .*

From the depths of Mr. Wilbur's throat came a low gasp as he pulled away the last bit of paper. Cradled in his hands was a small, rounded cylinder of reddish-brown. It was covered in the tiny strokes and dashes of a forgotten language.

Abby breathlessly leaned closer. "An ancient artifact," she whispered, her throat dry. "Who can know where it came from?"

"Babylon, or Assyria, or Persia, maybe," Mr. Wilbur muttered.

"This may be an invaluable piece of history," Mr. Baker said.

The others weren't quite as transfixed. "What else is in the crate?" Seth asked.

Mr. Wilbur leaned down to pick up another item when Phil suddenly put a hand on his father's arm. Mr. Baker was surprised to see his son staring rigidly to the left, and turned to see what the matter was. He stiffened.

"Don't move!" came a menacing cry. Three men, their faces covered by balaclavas and sunglasses, were advancing towards them.

CHAPTER 15

M r. Wilbur immediately swung the cylinder behind his back and straightened up, putting his hand protectively on John's shoulder.

"What are you doing on my land?" he challenged.

Phil sneaked his fingers into his pocket and then slowly behind his back, gripping his iPhone tightly. To his surprise, he felt someone pressing a cold, smooth object into his other hand. He glanced quickly at his father. *The car key*?

"You will come to no harm if you do as we say," the leader of the men replied.

Phil swiped his thumb across his iPhone's screen, hoping to unlock the phone, and then estimated where the "emergency call" option would be. Beads of perspiration appeared on his forehead. He would have to dial 911 with no point of reference, and suddenly found himself wishing he had a good old "brick" with buttons rather than a touchscreen marvel.

"What are you doing on my land?" Mr. Wilbur repeated, flinching as one of the thugs brandished a revolver.

The man made no reply as he looked down the cellar hole and into the crate.

Mr. Wilbur's grip on John's shoulder was tightening as he watched the proceedings, and he forgot about the cylinder in the other hand as he brought it forward.

The thug caught sight of it, and his tone hardened. "Wait—you've already found what's in the crate?" He waited in a sinister pause. "That's too bad." He pulled the hammer back and took aim at Mr. Wilbur.

In the twinkling of an eye, Mr. Baker had yanked out and cocked his own pistol, yelling, "Drop it!"

The thugs were caught off guard and gave a start of surprise at the sight of the weapon. The other man immediately swerved the barrel and fired at the new threat, but by providence the bullet glanced off Mr. Baker's pistol. His own shot went wide.

"Now, Phil!" Mr. Baker bellowed as he dashed towards the trespassers. He tackled the leader and they both wrestled furiously while Mr. Wilbur rushed at the other two thugs.

Phil's heart was in his throat, but he knew what he had to do.

"Everyone! Get in the car!" he ordered, grabbing John and Abby's hands and almost dragging them to the car in his haste.

Emily, Seth, and Andy were close behind. All clambered inside, and Phil shoved the key into the ignition, his heart pounding. A bullet zipping a few inches wide of the window told him their attempted escape had not gone unnoticed. Nobody was supposed to get away. Phil knew he was the target.

He slammed on the accelerator, and the car hurtled over the humps and bumps of the field. Another bullet followed them, screaming over the roof.

"Stay down!" Phil yelled, fearing for their lives. They were almost safely around a hill. *Just a few more seconds . . .*

Despite Phil's warning, Emily stole one last glance out the rear window and let out a shriek. "Dad! Daddy! He's been shot, he's been shot! Oh, no! Oh, no! Oh, no!"

"Are you sure?" Phil demanded.

"Where was he hit?" Andy pressed, but nothing intelligible could be deciphered from Emily's hysterical cries.

Seth spoke not a word.

Phil did not slow down, but kept a speedy course for the house. He caught Abby's glance in the rear-view mirror. Her eyes were full of fear, of shock, of terrified uncertainty. It was a glance that echoed, to his very core, the flood of confusing emotions that blinded and deafened him. His movements were reflexive, as though detached from his mind's control. *House. Get back to the house. Somehow, anyhow.* That was all that mattered.

****

"So that's when Charles and I decided to move to our farm," Mrs. Baker finished, stirring sugar into her tea.

"That's a pretty amazing story," Mrs. Wilbur said. "Growing up in England must have been such an experience for you—and I guess that explains why you like your tea hot!"

Mrs. Baker nodded with a laugh.

Mrs. Wilbur began clearing the kitchen. "Well, Jed hasn't phoned yet, so I suppose he doesn't need us to bring anything. I'm sure they'll be starving when they come back."

"I wonder how they're getting on," Mrs. Baker said, picking up a tea-towel as her friend plunged her hands into the hot, sudsy washing-up water. "Maybe we should ask if they want us to bring lunch to them."

"That's an idea. Oh, and please don't forget to give me that recipe for coffee and walnut brownies. The kids really—" she broke off as she glanced out the window in front of her. Her eyes grew wider the longer she stared. "Look!" She pointed, her hand dripping with soap.

Mrs. Baker followed her friend's motion and froze. Far in the distance, getting smaller every moment, was a white helicopter.

"I have to phone Jed!" Mrs. Wilbur cried, grabbing a towel.

"I'm going to call the police!" Mrs. Baker rushed to her purse.

Minutes later, when Mrs. Baker hung up, Mrs. Wilbur said, "I tried and tried to get hold of Jed, and I just couldn't! I even tried to call Charles and Phil, but that didn't work either."

Mrs. Baker shook her head. "I didn't think it would. I just pray our families aren't in danger."

"Danger!" Mrs. Wilbur repeated in shock. "What about the kids?"

"Hannah, I don't know." Mrs. Baker placed a hand on Mrs. Wilbur's shoulder. "The Lord will protect our loved ones. He's done it many times before, even when we haven't noticed. 'I will say of the Lord, "He is my refuge and my fortress; my God, in Him I will trust."' Let's—"

She was interrupted by a determined banging on the front door.

"I'll get it!" Mrs. Wilbur called, just as Laura had reached for the handle. The young girl drew her hand away as her mother peered through the eye hole.

Mrs. Wilbur gasped in relief and yanked the door open. "Kids! You had us worried! Lunch is—"

A cold hand gripped Mrs. Baker's heart as she caught sight of Phil's face. "Where's Father?"

Phil swallowed, his hair disheveled and his eyes filled with worry. "I don't know. The trespassers could have taken him, or he might be. . ." He did not finish the sentence. He didn't want to.

Emily broke into sobs and rushed to Mrs. Wilbur.

"Emily, what is it?" Mrs. Wilbur asked. "What happened? Emily? Emily, tell me!"

Emily let out a hiccupped sigh and endeavored to breathe slowly. "Daddy," she moaned. "He was—he was—oh-ohhh!" She lost control and started blubbering again.

Mrs. Wilbur looked helplessly up at the other children as she caressed the sobbing girl in her arms. Tom and Zachary, who had hurried over as soon as they heard the commotion, stood near Laura. The three of them were scared by the others' reactions, their fear heightened by the fact that they had no idea what was going on.

Laura started stroking Emily's arm. "It's okay, it's okay," she said, trying to sound reassuring but failing. "Why are you crying?"

"Emily said Dad was shot," John answered for her.

Mrs. Wilbur gave a startled cry. "Shot? Is he all right?"

"I—I don't know," John replied.

"I think Emily was the only one who saw," Abby said. Her face was ashen and her lips drawn in a straight line.

"Emily," Mrs. Wilbur said in a serious tone, "I need to know what happened. Where was Dad hit?"

Again Emily tried to regulate her breathing. When it was quite steady, she began, "I looked out of the rear window, and saw—and saw Daddy and Mr. Baker being marched off at gunpoint. Dad was holding his arm, and his sleeve was all red and . . . red and . . ." That was the last anybody heard as Emily's words smudged into incomprehensible wails.

"So it was Dad's sleeve that had blood on it?" Mrs. Wilbur broke in.

Emily nodded.

"Anything else?"

Emily thought for a moment, then shook her head. "No," she stammered. "That was all."

Mrs. Wilbur let out a long breath of relief, and Mrs. Baker took the opportunity to ask some questions of her own.

"Was Father hurt?" she asked immediately.

"Not that I could see," Phil said. "It all happened so fast. Emily, you said both of the fathers were marched off. Did our father look okay?"

"I—I didn't see anything—anything wrong."

"Thank the Lord," Mrs. Baker said quietly.

Mrs. Wilbur frowned in indignation and concern. "Jed needs to be nursed! Will he be all right? Why did those criminals take him with them?"

"I have no idea, Mrs. Wilbur." Phil shook his head.

"Will he be all right?" she asked again.

Phil paused for a moment before replying. "I know my father will do all he can to help your husband, Mrs. Wilbur, and he's a good medic."

The police arrived shortly thereafter and the whole story was poured out. Though the children were still shocked, their minds had cleared somewhat and they were able to recall the main details.

"So there were three trespassers?" the police officer asked after awhile.

"Yes, sir," Phil said.

"And you said you saw a helicopter fly away from the property?"

"Yes, we saw it."

"So did we," Mrs. Baker added.

"Could somebody please lead us to the location this happened?"

Phil glanced at his mother, and then nodded. "I'll go."

"I'll come too," Andy said.

They stood up and left the house, and as they did so Emily started sniffing. "I don't want to go to that place ever again. I'm scared."

"I'm scared too," Laura agreed.

Zachary's eyes were round. "I'm altho thcared," he lisped.

"I'm scared of this farm!" Emily continued. "I don't want to live here! I want to go back to our real home!"

Mrs. Wilbur sighed as all her children, even Seth and John, gathered around her. "Now, now," she mumbled, but Abby could see that her eyes were very wet.

At another time, Abby would've felt sad that her friends wanted to move away, but at that moment she understood perfectly. The situation looked very bleak. *Here we are*, she thought. *Our fathers have been captured by thugs, we don't know if they're okay or where they are, we're entrenched in a mystery that is getting increasingly dangerous, we can't solve it, and we're frightened. It's like a nightmare—but we're awake, and we're living it.*

Mrs. Baker was the first to overcome her emotions and concentrate on the others. "I'm sure you won't want to spend the night here alone," she said. "Would you like to stay at our house?"

Mrs. Wilbur pinched her lips together, unable to speak, and nodded gratefully.

****

As the police officers walked past the Bakers' car, Phil pointed out the long scrape where the bullet had just missed lodging in the roof.

"It's a mercy none of you were hit," an officer said. "You said the men shot at you twice?"

"That's right," Phil replied.

"Nice folks," Andy managed dryly.

The boys slipped into one of the police cars and directed the way to the location of the last crate, where the Wilburs' car still stood, looking strangely out of place.

They all got out, heading straight for the cellar. It was empty.

"The thugs must have taken the crate with them," Phil muttered in disappointment.

"You said ancient artifacts were in it," the officer said. "Do you have any idea how they might have gotten here?"

"No," Phil said quickly, but then a thought struck him. It apparently occurred to Andy too, because he was the one to speak.

"Well, I can think of a link. Mr. Larone, one of the men to claim the ring, had a grandfather who was an archeologist."

One of the officers noted that down on a pad of paper, saying that was a clue that deserved some looking into. Then Phil re-enacted the scene. The officers scoured the area and found traces of blood which were probably from Mr. Wilbur's arm.

"We saw a helicopter appear behind that hill and fly away," Phil finished.

"This hill?" the officer said. "Then let's see what we find. Please stay here with my colleagues; the situation might still be dangerous."

Phil and Andy did as they were told, staying with two men while the other two cautiously rounded the hill. They returned within a few minutes, saying they had searched for clues, only finding patches of flattened grass where the helicopter must have landed.

"Do you think those men will come back to this farm?" one officer asked.

"I don't, sir. My youngest brother heard Mr. Larone refer to this as 'the last crate,' and I believe it is." He had already told the men the other reasons they had for suspecting the old man, including Tom's accidental overhearing of his phone call.

"We're going to do all we can to investigate Mr. Larone's possible involvement in this case," the officer said, "and find out where Mr. Baker and Mr. Wilbur were taken. We'll get a detective to work on the case; he will probably come by soon to ask a few questions."

"A detective? Good." Phil breathed in relief. "I look forward to meeting him. I'm sure he'll spot any clues we missed and find our fathers much sooner than we ever could by ourselves."

CHAPTER 16

"Good afternoon, I'm Detective Clement Gray," the man said in a nasal voice as he greeted Mrs. Baker and then shook Phil's hand later that day. "I need to ask you, Philip, a few questions about what happened."

"I'd be happy to answer them, Detective, and I'm pleased to meet you," Phil replied as he and Mrs. Baker led the man to the living room and offered him a seat. The twins and Tom followed.

Detective Gray sat back and took a deep breath, folding his hands on his belly. "First of all, I heard about this tragedy, and I extend my sympathy and deepest condolences for your loss."

Phil blinked and Mrs. Baker started back in surprise. "Excuse me?" she said.

"Your loss," Detective Gray repeated. "Your husband is lost."

"Oh, well yes, but he's not—he's not—"

"I think my mother means that condolences aren't necessary," Phil said.

"Precisely." Mrs. Baker nodded vigorously. "And besides, with your help he won't be lost for long."

The detective chuckled. "That's very kind of you. I'm flattered."

Andy frowned. *Flattered? Did he just take that as a personal compliment?*

"Now, to business," Detective Gray said, clearing his throat. "What were you all doing when the trespassers arrived?"

"Well," Phil began, "we were looking beneath the cellar for an old crate we thought the criminals might be after. They had removed two from the property already, and we wanted to discover what was inside them."

Detective Gray nodded slowly. "How did you know where to look?"

"It's quite a long story," Phil replied, trying to think of a concise answer.

"I have time." Detective Gray smiled, leaned back, and twiddled his thumbs.

Abby wondered why he didn't seem to have a notepad, and decided he must have a very good memory not to need one.

Phil plunged into the story, telling the detective all about the ring, the history of Hank and Victor, and Mr. Larone's riddle. As he spoke, he couldn't help noticing the man's balding, dull brown hair, round, button nose, spindly limbs, and potbelly. "We figured out where to look, and unfortunately weren't able to retrieve the last crate before the trespassers arrived."

"Hmm. Interesting. Philip, are you at university?"

Phil floundered for a moment at the unexpected question. "Er, I'm studying through a correspondence course and learning the skill of invention from my father." His eyebrows lowered. "I'm sorry, but I'm not sure what that has to do with finding him."

"Oh, yes, well, of course you'd be wondering that. I'm just pleased you're available to help us solve the mystery. Now—" Detective Gray paused, as though trying to pick up a train of thought. "Ah, yes. My next question. I was told there was some shooting going on. Why did Charles bring a gun with him?" His eyes were narrowed almost in suspicion as he waited for Phil's answer.

"We knew there was a possibility the trespassers would arrive before we got the crate back to the house, so my father brought his pistol as a precaution."

"A precaution! Interesting. I heard that he shot at the trespassers; is that right?"

"That was only once they shot at us." Phil's brow furrowed as he tried to remember the exact sequence of events. "It all happened very fast. They arrived, threatened us with a gun, and my father pulled his out in order to warn them. Then," he said, his speech slowing, "when they realized that we already knew what was in the crates, the leader prepared to shoot. Our father returned fire, and then he and Mr. Wilbur rushed at the trespassers to enable us to get away." He gave the twins a look of triumph. "So that's why the criminals took our fathers, and tried to prevent us from escaping!"

"Why?" Abby asked.

"Because we knew what was in the crate!" Phil exclaimed.

"That's right!" Andy snapped his fingers. "Just before the leader took aim, he said something like, 'It's too bad you know what's in the crates.' But if it was so important that nobody find out, why did the thugs let our fathers live?"

Phil didn't answer.

"Maybe they don't plan to let them live," Abby said quietly.

"Er—ahem," Detective Gray broke in, seemingly unsettled that he was not the one doing the questioning. "Tell me, er, about the ring. I heard there was a rumor that it might not have been stolen."

"Not?" Mrs. Baker said in surprise. "Then what happened to it?"

"Well, the rumor goes that Mr. Wilbur hid the ring so that he could keep it."

"Oh, that can only be gossip," Mrs. Baker said quickly. "There's nothing whatsoever to back it up."

"Yes," Phil added. "We *know* he's innocent, and his capture only proves it."

"I seem to have found something you feel strongly about," he replied with a condescending smile. "Unfortunately, that is often a problem. Criminals can disguise themselves very well, and one can never be too sure who to trust. Even a quiet, kindly neighbor can turn out to be a wanted thief."

"It's outrageous to suspect Jed Wilbur of criminal activities!" Mrs. Baker exclaimed.

Her children looked up quickly. For her to forsake quiet politeness and speak with such bold, yet respectful, firmness was unusual. It might have been a topic she was particularly struck by, or perhaps the final blow to break the dam of accumulated emotion, but she spoke passionately and decisively.

"Why, you're recommending holding suspicions towards anyone and everyone—as though they're all guilty until proven innocent! That is not justice!"

Detective Gray was just as taken aback, and did not reply.

"We would all agree that Jed has done absolutely nothing to put doubts in our minds as to his character," Mrs. Baker continued. "By contrast, Mr. Larone's behavior has been consistently suspicious and we have found *many* reasons to question his character. The phony note he buried, the matching tire tracks on the farm, and his phone conversation all point to him as the one we should be suspecting."

"Er, uh," the detective stammered, "no need to worry—*of course* we are looking into all that. I just want to know more about Mr. Wilbur so I can get an understanding of why he was taken."

Phil groaned inwardly and tensed his jaw. *We don't have to know* why *he was taken—we need to know* where *he was taken!*

Detective Gray glanced at his watch. "I should probably get going soon. My workday is almost over and I have to go to the office before heading home."

Abby's eyes widened in dismay. "Detective, when can we expect to have some idea of my father's whereabouts? We are extremely anxious about him."

"Of course you are, of course you are. Well, I've got a great deal of leads to follow up on, and this case sounds like a complicated one. I can't give you an exact estimation of the time I'll need. Each case is different."

"Sir," Phil said, a sense of urgency in every word, "the lives of two upright men are at stake here. The criminals are dangerous men, and they need to be caught."

Detective Gray nodded and finally managed to heave himself off the sofa.

"You're a smart young man, Philip," he said, an ingratiating grin lifting his ponderous cheeks as he shook Phil's hand. "You really shouldn't waste your brain on correspondence courses. Mrs. Baker, it was a pleasure to meet you."

They followed him to the door, said polite goodbyes, and then Phil shut the door and leaned against it.

Abby let out a long sigh, an exasperated look on her face.

Phil nodded, understanding his sister's sentiment.

"What made him keep referring to your education?" Abby asked. "It's completely unrelated to Father's location!"

"We had to defend Mr. Wilbur as if we were his lawyers!" Andy said.

"Easy does it," Phil cautioned. "He's probably a fine detective." He, too, let out a sigh. "He's just not Detective Mortimer."

****

The Wilburs were settling into the Baker house, taking up the same rooms as their previous sleepover, when the doorbell rang. Andy went to open the door.

"Oh! Hello Mr. and Mrs. Hill—please come in," he welcomed. The Hills were longstanding friends of the Bakers.

"Thank you, Andy," the senior gentleman replied. He held a large basket under his arm.

"We're so sorry to hear about your father," Mrs. Hill added as she stepped inside.

"Yes, and we called earlier to ask your mother if she'd like to borrow Flurry for awhile," Mr. Hill said, motioning to the beautiful Border Collie at his side. "Can she come in?"

"Oh, yes, that's fine." Andy nodded eagerly and turned to his little brother. "Tom, please tell Mother that Mr. and Mrs. Hill are here. Thanks."

He shook hands to welcome both visitors, and then Mr. Hill led Flurry into the house and set down the large basket.

A smile lit up Andy's face. "Hello, Flurry, old girl!" He dropped to his knees to ruffle her thick, black-and-white coat. The Wilbur children and the mothers were soon on the scene.

There were warm greetings, and then Mrs. Hill said, "We're very sorry to hear about Charles and Jed, and wanted to know if there's anything we can do to help?"

"Thank you," Mrs. Baker replied sadly, "I think we'll be fine once everybody's settled in. That is, as fine as possible."

"Just let us know if there's anything you can think of," Mrs. Hill insisted.

Mrs. Baker nodded. "Thank you. I've just got to keep reminding myself that the Lord is my refuge and my fortress, and I have to trust in Him to work things out."

Mrs. Wilbur let out a little sob, her face creasing as she tried to keep back tears. Both Mrs. Baker and Mrs. Hill put their arms around her shoulders, and soon the three of them were in a group hug, praying, sniffing, and crying together.

". . . And Flurry likes a lot of exercise each day," Mr. Hill was saying to the gathered children, "so let her have a good run-around outside."

"Yes, sir, we will," Andy said.

"Of course, exercise makes her thirsty," Mr. Hill continued, "so what do you need to remember?"

"Water!" Laura and Tom chorused.

"Water!" Zac copied, a little late.

"That's right. Make sure she can always get to her bowl, and that it's always got water in it."

"Where will she sleep?" John asked.

"She can sleep indoors, in her basket." Mr. Hill motioned to the basket he had been carrying. "Her blanket and a tub of food is in there—who can remember how often to feed her?"

"Me, me! Ooh, I can!" Laura said.

"Me too!" Tom said.

"How often, then?"

"Twice a day!" they both said.

"Twithe!" Zac copied with a lisp.

The Hills stayed a little longer, and then they said goodbye to everyone and to Flurry, who seemed to understand what was going on.

"Not only is the dog a great protection," Mrs. Wilbur said, when the children were playing outside, "but she's also a great distraction for the kids."

Mrs. Baker nodded in agreement. "You're right. She'll be wonderful for taking their minds off things."

It was later that evening that the phone rang, and as nobody seemed to be getting it, Phil got up from his desk to answer.

"Hello, this is the Baker residence, Philip speaking."

"Why, hello, Phil!" came the reply in a neatly clipped British accent.

"Detective Mortimer!" Phil gasped. "You have no idea how glad I am to hear your voice."

"Likewise. Listen, I heard about your father and Jed Wilbur—that is a terrible business. I am working on another case right now, but from the sounds of it yours is very urgent, and I'd like to help."

"Thank you, Detective, thank you! The police are on the job and have sent their own detective to investigate, but I don't think he's the most—er— suitable person for the case."

"Whom did they send?"

"Detective Clement Gray. He came around today to ask me some questions."

"Clement Gr—no, I'm afraid he won't do. He is not suited to a case like this. I can't promise anything, but I'll do what I can and keep in touch."

CHAPTER 17

Mr. Baker slowly came around. His head was swimming, and he opened his eyes only to see dizzying blurs in the darkness. He blinked a few times, to no avail, and closed his eyes again to wait for his head to clear. He became increasingly aware that he was lying on a hard surface, and that the air was close. He sniffed, trying to grasp what scent was in the air. It reminded him of his workshop at home.

When his eyes eased open a few minutes later, he felt just as drowsy, and he wondered if he had dozed off. The world around him was dark and cool, and when he tried to turn over he got the sense of being uncomfortable and cramped, with his legs bent stiffly.

Incoherent thoughts sprang to his mind. "I've got to get up," he mumbled. "The twins must feed the horses. Phil must help me work on that invention. Jed needs help. Jed needs help?" He was more awake than before. "Jed needs help! Of course he does!"

He tried to sit up, wondering why it was so hard to lift himself, when he bonked his head against the low roof. "Ouch! Where am I?" he wondered aloud. He attempted to feel around him, but realized that his hands were tied behind his back. His ankles were bound too, but he still managed to move his legs around and bump them against the walls of his prison.

"Wood!" he muttered as he recognized the hollow sound. "At this shape and size, this must be a . . . a crate!" He suddenly realized why the smell reminded him of his workshop. The crate smelled of sawdust.

He wiggled his fingers in an effort to feel the ropes bound tightly around his wrists. Then he managed to carefully ease himself into a sitting position without banging his head again, pushing his feet against the wall at the end of the crate. From there he could see a tiny crack of light coming in through a gap around the top of the crate. He peered through the gap as closely as possible, but could not make out anything.

As he paused to consider the predicament, he suddenly noticed that all was quiet. There were no voices, no sound of footsteps, nothing. The chill in the air made him shiver. "Hello?" he said softly through the gap in the crate. "Is anybody there? Jed? Can you hear me?"

There was no reply. He shuffled his wrists and tensed his muscles, heaving and straining against his bonds. It was no use. Next, he decided to try to work on the ropes around his ankles. He shifted his weight, bending his knees as tightly as he could and reaching out beneath him with his hands until he touched the backs of his shoes. Gripping them, he tugged and pulled to get them off.

He had to stop, panting, every few minutes. Working in such a restricted space was extremely tiring, and Mr. Baker soon realized that the crack was allowing only a little oxygen inside.

"If it wasn't for that, I'd probably suffocate," Mr. Baker muttered. The crate was already very stuffy. He heaved himself back into a sitting position to gasp through the gap. "Jed? Are you here? Do you have enough air?" Still, there was no response. "Lord," he prayed anxiously, "what if Jed is in a crate that doesn't have a crack like mine? Please, please help me get out of here and find him. And please keep him safe!"

****

When Abby came downstairs early the next morning, she was surprised to see Phil in the living room, leaning over something he was studying on the table.

"Good morning!" she said.

He looked up in surprise. "Morning. What are *you* doing up so early?"

"I couldn't sleep anymore but didn't want to wake Emily and Laura, so I thought I'd read my Bible in here." She tapped the leather-bound volume under her arm. "I can't go ahead and feed the horses because the girls want to come too. What are you doing up so early?"

"Trying to figure out where Father and Mr. Wilbur were taken." Phil straightened and ran a hand through his hair. "Look Abs, the police are on the job, and so is Detective Gray, but I've got a feeling they're not going to crack the case anytime soon if we don't get involved."

"What about Detective Mortimer? You said he was going to help us."

"He's busy with another case, which he can't exactly drop no matter how much he'd like to. There's no telling how much time he'll have to spare on this."

"So we're going to do all we can," Abby said with a nod. "I agree." She came over to look at the map he had been poring over.

"The trespassers held us at gunpoint here." Phil tapped a point he'd circled on the map. "The helicopter was about here, and when it took off it headed northeast."

"Can't you find out who the helicopter belongs to, or who was flying it at the time? Won't there be a control tower somewhere that coordinates flights and landings, that would have that sort of information?"

"I'm not sure," Phil said. "If there was any chance of getting that kind of information, the police would have it by now. What about the crate? It must have been loaded into the helicopter, as I didn't see anything hanging under it."

"We could assume it was taken to the criminal headquarters," Abby thought aloud, "and that Father was too."

"Morning," Andy greeted as he came in. "I heard you two talking and wanted to find out what's up."

"We're figuring out where Father and Mr. Wilbur were taken," Phil said.

"I reckon the smartest thing to do is to follow Mr. Larone around," Andy said. "I'm sure he will lead us on to something."

"He's just had an accident and lost his car," Abby pointed out. "He can't go anywhere."

"True, but people can still visit him," Phil said slowly.

"We can't keep watch over his house all the time," Abby said. "How could we be sure not to miss anything?"

"We could set up a camera on his porch."

"That might look a little obvious, Andy, don't you think?" Phil countered.

"A small one wouldn't," Andy persisted. "We could buy a camera-trap that nature lovers set up when they want to spot rare animals. It's motion-sensitive, so it only switches on when something moves."

There was a pause, and then Phil nodded slowly. "I think you're on to something there. Do you think we could afford one between the three of us?"

"Yes, I'm sure we could," Andy said.

"Could we get it to live-stream to one of the laptops?"

"It's probably possible," Andy answered.

"How could we set it up without Mr. Larone noticing?" sensible Abby asked.

A mischievous grin spread over Andy's face. "I'm sure we'll think of something."

****

"Do you think he's home?" Abby asked Phil under her breath. The three of them were standing on Mr. Larone's porch, awaiting an answer to the doorbell. Almost two minutes had passed without a sign of the man's presence—no footsteps from inside, no rattle of a key in the lock, and not even a shadow over the peephole.

"I don't know," Phil admitted tensely. He thought of the small camera inside Abby's shoulder-bag, and was uneasy about their plan to distract the man so one of them could install it. The plan was simple. If Mr. Larone was home, Phil would offer to take him grocery shopping. The twins would volunteer to mow the front lawn in his absence, and have the opportunity to set up the camera. Deep down, Phil doubted Mr. Larone would go ahead with their suggestions, but it was the only plan they had been able to think of.

"Maybe he didn't hear the bell," Abby whispered. "Maybe you should ring again."

Phil, thinking hard about what he would say if the man opened the door,

160

reached out to press the button when Andy suddenly grabbed his arm.

"Wait!" he whispered. "Maybe it's better if we don't have to persuade Mr. Larone to go along with our idea."

"You mean we should set up the camera—now?" Abby asked softly.

Phil shook his head. "That's a bad idea. He could be looking out a window at us at this very moment."

Andy frowned in thought, his eyes wandering over the house and garden for an idea. Suddenly, his eyebrows shot up and he drew in a breath. "But he isn't!"

"He isn't doing what?"

"He isn't watching through a window—that is, I don't think he is," Andy whispered hurriedly.

"What do you mean? Why not?" Phil questioned.

"Look—the faucet is attached to the hose. It's leaking little drops of water. That means it's switched on, and that Mr. Larone is probably—"

"Watering his back garden!" Phil finished in surprise. "I think you're right! We have to find out exactly where he is. Stay here, and try not to look suspicious. I'll be back in a moment."

He stepped quickly off the porch and around to the faucet. As the twins watched, he followed the trail of garden hose to the corner of the house, and then paused and cautiously peered around it. Then he disappeared as he continued to follow the hose.

Phi was approaching a high wooden fence with a door to one side. It was slightly ajar. The hose snaked through the tiny gap in the doorway, and Phil's heart thumped faster as he realized what a vulnerable position he was in. Mr. Larone could be anywhere—more specifically, he could be on the other side of the door, about to walk through it.

Phil was aware of a faint rushing sound, no doubt that of the water streaming through the hose and blessing the garden with its life-giving drops. Swallowing his concerns, he squeezed as close to the side of the house as he could and slipped his fingers over the top of the fence. He placed one shoe against the fence, about two feet from the ground, and slowly levered himself up until he could just peer over the top.

Just a second-long glimpse satisfied his curiosity, and he eased himself quietly down before dashing back to the twins.

"He is in the garden," Phil said, hardly leaving gaps between his hasty words. "He's watering the plants in the flower-beds along the edges. You set up the camera—I'll watch him. If he comes close, I'll run back in time to warn you."

Andy nodded. "Okay. Quick, Abs, get the camera."

As Phil rushed out of sight again Abby threw open her bag and pulled out the device. "Where do we—"

"Let's put it here," Andy said, tapping a porch beam covered in ivy. As Abby held the camera in place, he pulled out a roll of sturdy tape and fumbled for the cut end.

"Why can I never find it?" he moaned in frustration, and then handed it quickly to Abby, who was better at doing that sort of thing. He held the camera in place for her while she ran her finger along the roll of tape and then began picking at a certain spot with her nails.

"Got it," she gasped, pulling out a length of tape.

"Put it around here first," Andy directed, "and mind the leaves. They can't look disheveled."

Abby did as he had said, trying to avoid ivy leaves as she secured the camera to the beam. A couple of strips of tape were needed, and her hurry was so great that she used her teeth to snip lengths off instead of bothering to use the scissors they'd brought.

The next moment, Phil appeared around the corner, dashing towards them at a remarkable speed. "He's coming!"

Abby was in the process of sticking down the last strip of tape, and a length remained unstuck. Her heart in her throat, she knew she could not leave the last bit loose or it would certainly be noticed. She hurriedly pulled it around the beam and smoothed it onto the front casing of the camera.

"Come on!" Andy said.

Phil looked alarmed. "We don't have a moment to lose!"

She snatched up her bag and joined the boys as they ran towards the car as fast as they could. She dived inside and shut the door just as Phil started the engine and pulled away. As they passed the corner of the house, Mr. Larone appeared around it. He was out of sight a moment later, being blocked by a leafy bush the car passed.

"Whew," Phil said, breathing a sigh of relief, "we made it in the nick of time."

Andy nodded, but Abby was thoughtful. "I just hope he doesn't notice that the last bit of tape is squashing some ivy leaves.

CHAPTER 18

"Oh, children!" Mrs. Baker breathed in relief as they arrived back at the house. "How did it go?"

"It was a close call, but we managed to install the camera just in time," Phil replied.

"Wow," Seth muttered as he and his siblings joined the group. "That must have been exciting."

"You said the camera you bought was motion-sensitive," Mrs. Wilbur said, "so it'll stay off until something triggers it, right?"

"Yes," Andy said. "Battery life will be preserved that way."

Phil had gone over to his laptop on the table to check on the live-stream he'd set up earlier, with some help from one of the employees at the camera store. "Nothing is showing at the moment," he announced. "I just hope it works. I was worried the ivy leaves might trigger it off constantly."

"We were careful about that when securing the camera," Abby said.

"Now, what if somebody does come to visit Mr. Larone?" Mrs. Baker asked. "What is your plan?"

"I'll drive over there to watch the proceedings," Phil said, "and follow if they go anywhere. I'll be keeping contact with you so that if anything suspicious crops up, you can tell the police where I am and what's going on."

"That sounds dangerous," Mrs. Wilbur said. "Shouldn't the police just follow right from the beginning and you all stay out of the way?"

"Unfortunately, the police are very busy as they are," Phil replied, "and they won't appreciate the false alarm if Mr. Larone is simply being taken for a drive by an old friend. I hope to check that out before asking for their assistance."

"I suppose you're right, Phil," Mrs. Wilbur agreed with a nod.

"Look! Look!" Abby suddenly cried, pointing frantically to the laptop screen. The others darted to see what was happening. Mr. Larone's porch was clearly visible, but because the camera was not very high on the railing, everything was being viewed from waist-height. The others watched as a pair of legs walked off the porch!

****

Mr. Baker ran his tongue over his dry lips, and then groaned as he got a cramp in his neck. He longed to stretch out and rub his sore shoulders, but that was impossible. He guessed it was the early hours of the morning, and he had not been able to sleep a wink all night.

He could hear no movement from the crate to his left, and sighed in relief. *Jed must be finally resting, or better yet, asleep,* he thought. Only about half an hour after he had woken up the previous day, he had called again through the crack and heard a very muffled moan. Feeling sure it was Mr. Wilbur, he kept on calling until the other had awakened enough to hold a conversation. From this Mr. Baker learned that his friend was also bound hand and foot in a similarly-sized crate, that it had a little hole in one wall, and that it seemed old and rickety. Despite Mr. Wilbur's pain and weakness, he was desperate to escape.

"You ask the Lord for an escape plan," Mr. Baker had said. "I'll try to get free so I can rescue both of us."

Whenever Mr. Wilbur had spoken that day, his voice had been faint and strained, as though he was talking through teeth clenched in pain. Throughout the night, both men had been shuffling and groaning uncomfortably.

Now that Jed's finally quiet, I'll try not to disturb him, Mr. Baker thought.

He turned his attention to the bonds around his ankles that he had been relentlessly trying to untie. The most progress had been achieved once he pulled his shoes off and managed to shift onto his stomach. From that position he was able to grasp his ankle bonds with his fingers and fiddle with the rope—until he got a calf-cramp, that is.

He shifted into that position again, trying to ignore the uncomfortable angle of his neck, and worked on the biggest knot of them all. He soon had to rest his aching limbs, and his mind began to wander. *How are Alice and the children? Are they safe? Have the police found Bud Larone guilty yet? Is there any way they could find out where we are?*

He thought about the likelihood of being rescued, and the difficulties involved in their location being discovered. Then he considered the possibility of Bud Larone getting away, and the thought snapped him back to action in working on the ropes.

Once I have my feet free, he told himself, *I can focus my attention on getting out of this crate. If I can just get out, I'm sure I'll be able to find a sharp edge somewhere to cut the rope around my wrists. From there I'll be able to consider the best way to get Jed to a hospital.*

He felt the knot just starting to give when the aching in his muscles could no longer be ignored. He swallowed in an attempt to wet his parched throat, and then frowned at the hollow growl of his stomach. *No water since yesterday morning. No food since yesterday, either. If these crooks don't look after us, we'll only survive until the end of tomorrow—and there's no telling if the police will find us by then. Besides, I'll soon be out of strength. As for Jed, well, he's already too weak to do much.*

Mr. Baker shuffled into a more comfortable position and tried to doze. When he opened his eyes again, the tiny streak of light from the crack seemed to be brighter, and he wondered how long he had been resting. A muffled cough told him that Mr. Wilbur was awake also.

"Jed?" Mr. Baker called softly. "Can you hear me?"

"Yes," was the faint reply.

"Have you been able to sleep?"

"Barely."

"How's your arm?"

"Very sore. Trying not to lean on it."

"I'm still working on that escape," Mr. Baker said, trying to sound optimistic.

"I'm still praying."

Mr. Baker again shifted to work on the ankle bonds. To his joy, the biggest knot came undone, but he knew that plenty of tight, little ones were left.

His right thigh suddenly tensed up in a cramp, and he dropped the rope and relaxed his muscles, grimacing as he waited for the pain to ease. Despite the pain, he heard a sudden, harsh sound, like that of a door being unlocked, and then came the sound of footsteps across a smooth, hard surface. He was immediately alert, and he strained his ears. *Could that be the police? Have they come to rescue us? If so, we need to attract attention. If not . . .*

He shuffled into a sitting position as quickly and quietly as he could, and peered through the crack. He could see nothing, so put his ear to the gap instead. He could hear nothing but more footsteps. *Maybe Jed can see who it is.*

"Jed?"

"Shhh!"

As Mr. Baker listened, the footsteps ceased and were replaced by the sound of muffled conversation. He only managed to catch a few words of the exchange.

"You know what . . . Boss . . . do . . ."

". . . Course . . . set up the . . . then boom."

"Does . . . destroy . . . ?"

"We'll . . . careful . . . dynamite. Nobody . . . notice!"

Mr. Baker froze as one set of footsteps began again. *Did I hear right? Boom, destroy, dynamite—there's only one thing that could mean! Oh Lord, please let me be wrong!*

When the second set of footsteps died away and the bolting sound was repeated there came the quiet call of, "Charles?"

"Yes?"

"Did you hear that?"

"Not too well, but I think I know what's going on."

"I could hear pretty well through the hole in my crate. They're going to set up dynamite and destroy this place. It's going to explode!"

****

"Somebody just walked away from Mr. Larone's house!" Abby exclaimed. "Before you arrived, I saw the legs approach the front door, and now they're going away again!"

"Oh, no, why didn't you set the camera higher?" Mrs. Baker moaned. "We're not going to recognize anybody this way!"

"We were in too much of a hurry to think that through," Andy said in disappointment.

"Why didn't the visitor go inside?" Emily muttered.

"Maybe Mr. Larone took too long to answer," Seth suggested.

"Wait a second." Phil shook his head. "I think I recognize that person."

"By his legs?" Seth asked incredulously.

"Not exactly. Didn't you notice the bag hanging at his waist?"

"You mean the tiny slip of color that you guess is a bag," Andy said.

"A bank robber!" Abby gasped.

"No," Phil replied, stifling the urge to laugh, "the postman!"

The others groaned as they realized Phil was right. "That explains why he just walked up to Mr. Larone's door and went back again," Emily said.

"And the way you could 'recognize' his pants and shoes," Seth added.

"If you ask me," Mrs. Wilbur said, "anything suspicious is going to happen at night."

"You're probably right," Phil agreed.

Mrs. Wilbur and the younger children had gone outside to play with Flurry when the doorbell rang.

"I'll get it, Mother," Phil said as he stepped forward protectively. "We can never know who it might be these days."

He peered through the peephole, then swung the door open in surprise. "Detective Mortimer! Please, come in!"

"Thank you, Phil. It's good to see you again."

"And you too—we weren't expecting you to come today."

"No; I am sorry I didn't call. I was in the area and found myself with a bit of time to spare."

The twins, Emily, and Seth heard Phil's delighted cry and came rushing to the door. Sure enough, there stood the wiry detective, his reddish-brown hair neatly combed from his high forehead and his mustache trimmed.

After exchanging greetings with Mrs. Baker and the twins, Detective Mortimer was introduced to Emily and Seth.

"Pleased to meet you both," he said politely as he shook their hands.

Emily couldn't help noticing the Englishman's perceptive eyes and prominent cheekbones, while Seth was amazed at the firm grasp of the unassuming man.

"Would you like a cup of tea?" Mrs. Baker asked as Phil was about to lead Detective Mortimer to the living room.

"Why, yes please!"

"What kind would you like?"

"Earl Grey, if you have any. Thank you."

"Mrs. Wilbur is looking after the children outside," Abby said. "I'll go call her."

"First of all, I am sorry to hear about what happened to Charles and Jed," Mortimer said, once he'd been introduced to Mrs. Wilbur and they were all settled in the living room. "Knowing your family, however—" he paused and looked at Phil. "You won't have been idle."

"That's right." Phil nodded. "We couldn't help ourselves." He quickly filled Mortimer in on Andy's idea of the camera-trap, and the way they had gone about installing it.

The detective smiled, but his face grew quickly sober. "That was a good idea, and I take my hat off to you for managing to pull it off. But I wouldn't recommend any more visits to that house. Mr. Bud Larone might be a more dangerous man than you think."

"Dangerous?" Mrs. Baker drew in her breath sharply.

Mortimer nodded. "Phil, I expect you will keep a close eye on that camera feed, and I would very much appreciate you letting me know if you see anything suspicious."

"I'd be glad to," Phil responded.

Mortimer took a sip of hot tea. "Now, there are a few things I wanted to ask you. Firstly, how many trespassers accosted you?"

"Three," Phil answered.

"Could you describe any of them?"

"Oh! Well, they were all strong men, I'd guess under the age of . . . fifty."

"More like under forty," Andy put in.

"I heard something about Mr. Larone's tire-tracks matching the ones near the location of the cellar," the detective said. "Could you please explain your theory behind that?"

"I think Mr. Larone must have driven to the cellar in order to make the measurements to the other crates," Phil said. "He could have got his car in through the gate at the other end of the farm."

The children then filled the detective in on the series of events, trying to describe everything in as much detail as their memories could muster. Detective Mortimer's face had upon it an expression of fixed concentration, as though he was soaking up every word. Abby noticed that he, like Detective Clement Gray, did not have a notebook. Unlike Detective Gray, however, Abby knew that he had an incredibly sharp memory and a keen grasp of detail.

Finally, Emily told what she had seen as they raced away in the car. Mortimer's brow creased. He asked about the position of Mr. Wilbur's bullet wound, which Emily didn't see, the size of the crate, and the direction of the helicopter's retreat. When he was satisfied with all of the answers, he stood up and drained the last sip of tea from his cup.

"Thank you all very much for your help," he said. "I trust it will not be long before this matter is all settled. I have a feeling it will reach its climax soon, and would advise you all to be ready for anything."

CHAPTER 19

A sudden burst of adrenalin coursed through Mr. Baker's body as Mr. Wilbur's last words rang in his ears.

"Smithereens!" Mr. Baker muttered incredulously. "If we don't get out of here in time, we'll be blown to smithereens! Jed, this is terrible."

"I know. How much time do you think we have?"

"I can only guess. One thing is for sure, though, and that is as long as I have strength left I'm going to use it."

"Me too," Mr. Wilbur replied with a tone of resolve. "I can't work on my bonds like you can, but I'll see how firm these walls are. This is a definite matter of life and death."

Both men hushed to silence as they busied themselves with their escape attempts. As Mr. Baker again worked his fingers against the harsh rope, he could hear Mr. Wilbur thumping about inside his crate. Mr. Baker thought it sounded like his friend was checking all the panels to discover the weakest one.

They did not speak again for the next half-hour, any moment of silence having the express purpose of resting weary muscles and inhaling lungfuls of air. Finally, Mr. Baker had to stop. His empty stomach ached worse than before, his tongue was starting to stick to the roof of his mouth, and his muscles were trembling from exertion and weakness.

Mr. Wilbur's crate was quiet too, and Mr. Baker was sure he was just as exhausted.

"Any success?" Mr. Baker asked faintly.

"Not yet. But I have found the weakest panel."

"That's something."

"And you?"

"Been working on one of the last knots," Mr. Baker replied. "The rope is so coarse I'm going to have blisters on my fingertips."

There was silence for awhile, until Mr. Wilbur said, "Charles?"

"Yes?"

"Do you think that detective friend of yours will get involved to try find us?"

"Probably."

There was a pause. Then Mr. Baker spoke again. "Anybody who comes to find us is in danger of those explosives." His throat went tight as another thought struck him. "And if Detective Mortimer comes to rescue us, Phil will almost certainly be with him."

****

Phil's eyelids drooped and he began to breathe deeply when the nodding of his head jerked him back awake. He shifted upright in his seat, folded his arms, and blinked hard in an effort to fend off fatigue. He looked wistfully over at Andy, Seth, and John sleeping peacefully around him in his room, and then forced his eyes back to the laptop screen.

The boys had agreed to take shifts that night in watching the feed of the camera-trap in case somebody came to visit Mr. Larone. Seth had volunteered to take first watch, from nine p.m. to twelve midnight, Phil had taken from midnight to three a.m., and Andy had chosen three to six a.m. Since John was the youngest, the others had offered for him to watch from six to nine a.m. Phil had been sure he would be wide awake during John's turn, but as the night wore on, he became less certain. He stifled a yawn and glanced at the time. *2:35 a.m.*, he thought. *Another twenty-five minutes to go.*

He pulled up a game of Spider Solitaire, keeping the blank feed visible on one side of the screen. *No point in me falling asleep. I may as well do something to keep my mind busy.*

He had just finished his second game and was about to switch to chess when he suddenly noticed the feed image flicker. Immediately alert, he checked it in full screen. Sure enough, there was a faint outline of light as Mr. Larone's front door opened. Phil could just make out two pairs of silhouetted legs against the soft light, and then both disappeared as the door closed and the screen was plunged into blackness again.

"Andy!" Phil whispered, leaping off his chair and rattling his brother's shoulder. "Andy, wake up!"

Andy groaned groggily. "Okay, okay, you can stop shaking me. Is it my turn to watch?"

"No. I've just seen someone at Mr. Larone's house and I need to call Detective Mortimer right away."

"Really?"

"Yes!" Phil exclaimed, darting back to the desk and picking up his phone. Moments later he was explaining the situation to the detective. Andy sat up and was almost fully awake.

"That's right. See you there—goodbye!"

Phil hung up and hurriedly pulled on a pair of socks. "We're closer to Mr. Larone's than the detective is, so I'm leaving now to see what's going on. If anyone leaves the house, I'll follow and keep the detective posted on where to go."

"Can I come too?" Andy asked, trying to conceal his hopeful plea in a nonchalant voice. "I mean, remember the last car chase?"

Phil's mind raced back to the time he and Andy had been pursuing kidnappers. "Yes, you pretty much saved the day that time. I don't know. I'll ask Mother."

Phil hurried quietly down the corridor and tapped on his parents' ajar bedroom door. "Mother?" he whispered, pushing the door open further. "Mother, I have to go now."

He found Mrs. Baker on her knees beside her bed, and guessed that she had fallen asleep while praying. She stirred, quickly catching the meaning of Phil's hurry, and turned on the lamp. "Yes, you'd better go right now. But Phil, please be careful."

"I will, Mother. Can Andy come along?"

As if on cue, Andy appeared in the doorway wearing a dark hat and jacket, his flashlight in one hand.

Mrs. Baker swallowed hard, her face worried and tired. "Boys, Detective Mortimer said Bud is dangerous. I can't bear the thought of you getting harmed."

Andy lowered his eyes, rubbing his ear casually to hide his bitter disappointment. "I guess I'll . . . uh . . . keep an eye on that camera feed."

Mrs. Baker shut her eyes and sent up a quick prayer, and then took a deep breath. "I didn't say you couldn't go, Andy. I just said I want you to be careful."

Andy's eyes shot up in plain surprise to meet hers. "I can go? Really? Thank you, Mother!"

"Phil, have you got your watch?" she asked suddenly.

"Oh, yes I do," he answered, pulling back his left sleeve. A question hovered around his eyebrows, but Mrs. Baker spoke again before he could voice it.

"I'll watch the camera-trap. Now go, and God speed!"

The boys hurried downstairs, where Phil slipped on a jacket and both of them tugged on their sneakers.

"Should we take Flurry?" Andy asked as they passed her basket. She was wide awake, her head erect as she watched the boys curiously.

"Uh," Phil hesitated for just a moment. "No," he decided. "We might need absolute silence."

"Oh, Phil, here's your phone," Andy said quickly. "You almost forgot it."

"Thanks! Have you checked the battery?" Phil grabbed the car-keys and stepped out the front door into the brisk morning air. He had to shut it carefully, as Flurry wanted to come too.

"Of course." Andy grinned in the darkness. "Half empty."

"Half full," Phil corrected. "You know, I'd better save power by disabling instant notification—"

Andy swung into the passenger seat and clipped on his seat belt. "Already done it."

"Wow—thanks!" Phil revved the engine. "Handy Andy."

They raced along the quiet roads, hoping they would not be too late. When they neared Mr. Larone's house, Phil switched off the headlights and engine, coasting silently down the lane. He pulled up a little way down from the house, where they had a good view of the front porch. A dark sedan was parked near it.

Phil quickly called Detective Mortimer to tell him they had arrived, and then the boys went quiet as they waited for something to happen. Seconds ticked by. Minutes passed. The boys' adrenalin had not worn off, and the waiting was terrible suspense. Phil began twiddling his thumbs and Andy tapped his fingers on his legs.

It was nearing 3:20 when Andy pointed down the road. "Look!"

"That must be Detective Mortimer," Phil said. "He's also driving without headlights or engine on."

They watched the small black Mercedes-Benz pull up near them, and recognized the detective as he looked over at them.

"Do you think we should go greet—" Andy stopped short as Phil suddenly tensed and stared in the direction of the house. Two shadowy figures were coming down the porch steps. One was heavyset with a lumbering stride, and the other was smaller and slightly stooped, with a stiff walk which the boys recognized. The dark sedan's lights flashed as the large driver unlocked the vehicle, and then both men climbed inside.

"Now what?" Phil wondered aloud, his voice tight. "Do we and the detective follow in separate cars?"

"I don't think it matters much, Phil, so long as we find out where they're going!" Andy replied.

The sedan's engine started up and it began purring down the road.

"Duck!" Phil commanded, hoping they had not been seen as the vehicle went right past the boys and Detective Mortimer.

"Follow them, Phil!" Andy burst out, watching as the vehicle slipped away.

"We have to wait for the detective to take the lead," he answered, fidgeting nervously with the steering wheel. "Besides, if we set off right away, they'll be sure to catch on that we're tailing them and all our work will be wasted."

Detective Mortimer was the first one to start off in pursuit, Phil following. Both left their headlights off, and as the boys stayed close behind the Mercedes, winding their way through town, Phil muttered, "I think they're heading to the freeway."

"I hope we haven't lost them," Andy said, unsettled by the fact that he couldn't see the sedan. "I'm sure we gave them too much of a head-start."

"The detective knows what he's doing."

Phil had been right—in a few more minutes they turned onto the freeway, and Detective Mortimer turned on his headlights. Phil did the same.

"Hey, this is the same freeway we thought Mr. Larone was heading for when he had his accident," Andy observed.

"Maybe we'll finally find out where he was heading."

"Do you think we should call the police?"

Phil thought for a moment. "What would we tell them? That we're following two people we suspect of criminal activities? We have no solid proof at all!"

"I guess you're right," Andy said.

A little later, Detective Mortimer called to ask if the boys were all right and to applaud them for spotting the action at Mr. Larone's house.

"I am not certain where the men are heading," he said, "but when they leave the freeway we're going to have to be careful. Follow my lead at all times. I'll call and tell you what to do."

The boys drove on in silence for another fifteen minutes before noticing that the Mercedes ahead was slowing. Without indicating, Detective Mortimer quickly turned off the freeway. The boys followed, finding themselves on a twisting, country road.

The detective called again. "This is the end of our chase," he said. "From here I can see where the sedan has parked. I'm going to pull off the road and turn my car around in case of an emergency getaway, and I'd recommend you do the same."

Phil did as he suggested, and then both boys emerged from the car feeling tense with excitement.

They joined the detective and walked briskly along the road, soon approaching an old warehouse. The sedan was in the parking lot.

"Have the men left their car?" Phil asked in a whisper.

The detective nodded. "They entered the warehouse through that door. I'm going to go first and check that the coast is clear."

They crept forward the last of the way to the warehouse, and then the boys stationed themselves around a corner while the detective slid soundlessly to the door, pausing in the shadows to watch and listen. He disappeared from the boys' view as he entered the building.

Phil looked down at his watch to check the time, and again the question flitted across his mind: *Why did Mother particularly ask if I had it on? Did she know I'd need it?* The question disappeared as quickly as it had come when Andy tugged on his elbow.

"Where's Detective Mortimer?" he whispered. "I thought he was going to come back and tell us to follow him."

"Maybe it's not safe yet," Phil replied, confident in the detective's abilities and wise judgment.

"What do you think this place is, anyway?"

"I've no idea. It might be Mr. Larone's headquarters."

"Do you really think he's the kingpin of the crate mystery?"

Phil shrugged. "I'm not sure, but he's definitely involved somehow. Remember what the detective said about him being dangerous? If we can catch Mr. Larone red-handed, well, that would be great. He might be involved in other criminal activities and could possibly give the police some clues."

"Hmm."

Again, the boys fell silent. Each moment felt like an age. They both felt the urge to relieve their inward restlessness through outward manifestations of it. Andy twisted and untwisted a short piece of string he found in his pocket. Phil repeatedly bit his lip and then absentmindedly felt for his pulse to try to measure his heart rate.

"It's been at least two minutes now," Andy said. "I really think something's happened."

"This is Detective Mortimer we're talking about," Phil answered, trying to quell his own uneasiness. "He's probably overhearing some very important information and will return as soon as he can."

By the time another minute had passed, Phil was beginning to feel just as restive as his younger brother.

"He was just checking that the coast was clear," Andy persisted. "What if he's been caught and needs us?"

"Andy! You're not helping!" Phil whispered in exasperation. "Here, take my phone. If I'm not back in five minutes—listen, five *whole* minutes—call the police. Can I borrow your flashlight?"

Andy handed it over, then watched as his older brother began creeping towards the entrance, trying to be as stealthy as the detective. Phil hovered around the ajar door and then stepped out of view. Andy checked the time on the phone. *4:01 a.m.*, he thought. *Battery level: still half empty. Five* whole *minutes to wait.*

The wind whistled through the branches of trees a little way away and blew against the old warehouse, making it creak. The moon disappeared behind some clouds, darkening the scene and making Andy shiver. He sighed, trying to slow the thumping of his heart. *Oh come on now, Andrew, pull yourself together! It's the first time you've been allowed to do something this thrilling and when you get back everybody's going to ask if you were scared. I'm brave, of course, but nobody really knows that yet.*

He was at that moment startled by a quiet thud around the other side of the building. *Calm down, calm down, calm down. It's just the wind.* He checked the time, feeling sure five minutes were almost up. He almost groaned. *4:02? Only one minute has passed? Oh Lord, please speed things up! I'm quite sca—*

or rather, I can't stand the—well, I really don't enjoy the tension. That is, I'm worried about Phil and Detective Mortimer. Please keep them safe, and help them catch Mr. Larone and his henchman.

He couldn't see any movement near the door, so he sat down in a small, shadowy recess to wait, trying to imagine what was keeping Phil so long. *He's probably sneaking around, spying on things and taking out bad guys. Oh, I wish I could too! Everybody's going to ask what I did. What can I say? 'I waited outside.' No, 'I kept watch.' Hmm. 'I stood guard.' That's better. Technically, I'm sitting guard, but I guess that doesn't count.*

A sudden sound caught Andy's attention. He froze. Hurrying footsteps were coming from the other side of the building, getting louder every moment. As the moon peeked out again, Andy could see two figures jogging towards him. "Phil and Detective—" he tried to mutter, but the sound stuck in his throat. In a moment, he recognized the two figures—one large and the other stiff—and they were striding straight towards him!

CHAPTER 20

Phil crept cautiously forward in the gloomy darkness of the warehouse. He was uneasy about switching on the flashlight until he knew it was safe to do so. Faint moonlight trickled in through gaps in the corrugated iron roof, outlining heaps of scrap metal and broken wood.

This place is a dump! Phil thought as he narrowly avoided tripping over a rusty pole. Where could the detective possibly be?

He knit his eyebrows and tried to blink the darkness away, scanning the place for any sign of life. He strained his ears for any whisper of sound, but his thumping heart was the loudest noise to be heard. The scene dimmed as clouds scuttled across the face of the moon, and Phil fumbled around clumsily.

"Detective?" he breathed. The building was eerily silent as he waited. "Detective?"

There was no reply. He paused for a few seconds, wondering if he should go back to Andy and call the police. They still had nothing to report about Mr. Larone, but the disappearance of the detective was very unsettling. He plucked up the courage to shine the flashlight, just for a split-second, around the building. The sudden light was a welcome relief from the gloom, but not one human being met his eyes. All he could see was heaps of odd scraps.

Just as he flicked the flashlight off and was turning to go, there was a quiet thud at the far end of the building. Then a faint shuffling began from somewhere nearby, coming nearer and nearer.

Phil froze. He wanted to run away, or shout, "Detective, is that you?" but knew that neither option was a good one.

"Phil?" came a whisper almost as quiet as a thought.

"Yes?"

The muted shuffle came even closer until there was a soft tap on his arm.

"Detective, you're safe! We didn't know what had happened to you," Phil breathed.

"Where's Andy?"

"Outside." Then he drew in a sharp breath. "I told him to call the police if I wasn't back in five minutes. He's going to start worrying about me."

"Then you had better go back and let him know we're both all right. I'm going to continue looking around. This would be the perfect place to hide two captured fathers."

****

Mr. Larone and his accomplice! What do I do? Andy thought frantically. *They'll catch me, and then who knows what will happen? But maybe they haven't seen me yet, and if I run now, they'll be sure to give chase—and I can't outrun that big guy! Maybe they won't see me. But then they'll get away! What if I trip them up as they pass and then sprint inside to find Phil? Will I manage it?*

The two men came ever nearer until the boy could hear their panting and clearly see their outlines. Fear overcame him and he sat rigidly, not daring to even breathe. His heart pounded in time to their steps, and he pressed his back hard against the wall of the recess.

"Got the detonator?" one voice said gruffly.

"'Course," the other replied.

They approached, and Andy almost burst with adrenalin as they seemed to slow near him. But they carried on, right past him, until they reached the dark sedan. Both of them collapsed inside the vehicle, the engine roared to life, and the car soon disappeared in the darkness.

Andy didn't move for awhile, his heart still thumping and his lungs burning for air. He gasped quickly and then rose unsteadily to his feet. He found himself staggering to the door, and had almost reached it when he realized he had meant to call the police if Phil didn't come back. He fumbled with the phone, seeing the time but not comprehending what he saw. It was at that moment that the ajar door eased farther open and Andy got a fright as he saw a person emerge.

"Andy?"

"Phil!" Andy gasped. "Phil, oh, Phil!"

"You haven't called the police yet, have you?"

"No. Oh, Phil, I was a coward! I let them get away!"

"Who? What are you talking about?"

"Mr. Larone. He and his crook came running right past me and I didn't do anything. I thought I was brave, but I'm not, and now they've got away!"

Phil stared at his brother in shock. "What are you saying? You mean Mr. Larone has already left?"

Andy nodded quickly, pointing to the empty parking lot.

"How strange," Phil muttered. "I guess we should give chase—maybe this warehouse was a false lead and they'll head to their real destination now."

"Yes, yes, let's fetch the detective and get out of here!" Andy gasped again as his older brother turned to the door. "Phil!"

"Yes?"

"I think I heard one of the men say 'detonator.'"

Phil looked stunned and horrified. "What?"

"Detonator. This place must be full of information they want to destroy—"

"Detonator! Andy, get away from here—NOW!" With that, Phil disappeared as he dived into the warehouse.

Andy was tempted to hesitate and warn Phil of the danger of going back, but knew he had better obey his brother. He started sprinting away from the building, each second dreading the sound of a tremendous "boom!" His thoughts whirled violently as he considered their predicament. *What if Phil doesn't make it out in time? What will I tell Mother? That I failed to stop those men when I could? No! I can't! Come on, Phil! Come on! Hurry up!*

He glanced back at the rickety building without slowing, with the result that he stumbled over some rough ground. Before he knew it, he had fallen into some grass beside a hedge. Feeling sure he was far enough away from the warehouse to be out of danger, he sat up and dusted himself off. Suddenly he stiffened as he heard the click of a car door being softly closed, then another.

"Why hasn't it blown up yet?" a voice gruffly asked.

Andy slowly turned his head. The sound had come from a gap in the hedge just a few paces to his left.

There came a mumbled reply.

"Someone must have made a mistake with the wiring," the first voice said. Andy recognized it as belonging to Mr. Larone.

"Not likely," the other voice said, a little louder. "Good thing those sneaks haven't noticed we're outside yet."

"Especially that Brit. He's been on my tail for years. I knew he was back on it when Len saw him visiting those Bakers. I thought he'd follow us tonight, and was proven right when I saw that Merc way behind us on the freeway."

Andy's blood ran cold as he realized what was happening. *This can't be just an attempt to destroy information. Far from it! These men know Phil and Detective Mortimer are inside! Yikes—this is a murder attempt! And if Phil and the detective don't get out in time, it'll probably be set up to look like an accident!*

The boy's head began to throb in time to the pounding of his heart, and his body began to shake. He squeezed his arms as tightly as he could, not noticing the pain. His eyes were glued to the warehouse. Every moment he felt a pang of fear for his brother. Every second he expected to see the place disappear in a shower of fire and shards. What could he do other than sit and wait? His mind was frantically searching for ideas but always coming to a blank.

It was in that moment that he became forcibly aware of two things, which he would later recall. First, he realized that he was afraid—not mildly anxious, not a little worried, not slightly concerned, but completely and thoroughly terrified. Second, and no doubt a main reason for the first, he realized just how small and helpless he was. No matter how fast he could run, or easily he could climb a tree, or skillfully he could play sports, or any of the other things he was proud of, nothing could erase the sickening feeling of being able to do nothing to change the nightmarish situation. His legs were limp. His arms were numb. His mind was blank. All he could do was stare.

Despite his deep despair, he subconsciously noticed the scene brighten as clouds revealed the moon once more. He could not shift his eyes from the warehouse, but his stare became a hollow one as his mind took notice of the light and the way it produced shadows. *Shadow of death. Where did that phrase come from? Of course. "Though I walk through the valley of the shadow of death, I will fear no evil; for You are with me . . ." You are with me. Lord, be with me! Be with Phil, please! Don't let him die. Nor the detective. I know I'm not very eloquent in prayers, but please, please help me to help Phil. I don't know what to do. I'm completely useless right now, and I know it. I'm too small to do anything on my own. Show me what to do. Please!*

"It's taking too long." Mr. Larone's voice interrupted Andy's prayer. "I'm not gonna wait anymore."

There was a grunt in reply, and Andy heard shuffling inside the car. His adrenalin mounted as he knew something dreadful would happen soon, and he'd have to be one step ahead of it.

He suddenly remembered that he still had Phil's phone. Easing onto his knees, he took it from his pocket and unlocked it, dialing 911. There would be no chance to speak to the police without the crooks overhearing, but perhaps the dispatcher would hear something that could alert him to the emergency. Feeling an urge to see what the crooks were up to, Andy gripped the phone in one hand as he crawled toward the gap in the hedge. He peered carefully around and saw the larger figure open a briefcase he'd placed on the vehicle's roof.

The moonlight outlined the man clearly as he took a remote-shaped object from the case.

"I'll give you a countdown," Mr. Larone wheezed.

What? Andy almost gasped. *A wireless remote? That must be what the crooks were referring to earlier! Lord, this is horrible! Show me what to do!*

****

189

Phil dashed back inside the rickety old warehouse and flicked on the powerful flashlight. *No more need for caution*, he thought as he beamed the light over heaps of rubbish.

"Detective!" Phil called. "Detective, where are you? We need to get out of here!"

He ran forward, dodging metal bars and broken crates. "Detective Mortimer! This place is going to blow up!"

"Phil! Over here!" came a muffled cry from the left.

"Where are you?" Phil shouted, racing along.

"Over here!" came the reply. "Under this stuff!"

Phil paused, trying to follow the voice as quickly as he could.

"I'm here," the detective continued, "near the wall. I was investigating an old grandfather clock, which was large enough to conceal a man, when I knocked over a sheet of corrugated iron. It fell on top of me, along with a whole lot of other debris. It's too heavy to shift alone."

"Are you under here?" Phil asked, rapping his knuckles against a sheet of metal covered in random scraps.

"Yes, yes!"

Phil propped the flashlight on a nearby mound and grabbed a broken plank, using it to forcefully shove away the scrap metal.

"It looks like the clock is holding you down," Phil said. He looked around and found a heavy rod that could pass as a crowbar. He slipped it under the great clock and pushed down with all his might. "I'm trying to lever it out of the way," he puffed under the strain.

"Right-o," the detective replied. "I'll help. Three, two, one, heave!"

The two of them worked together, Phil applying his weight to the lever and Detective Mortimer pressing up with all the force of his arms and legs from beneath the sheet of metal. With a moan, the grandfather clock lifted on one side and then rolled off with a crash. With the great hulk of weight gone, the detective could crawl out from under the corrugated sheet with a cough.

"We've got to go!" Phil cried, grasping the flashlight as he turned to head for the entrance. "It's going to explode!"

"Come on!" Detective Mortimer responded, heading in the opposite direction. "There must be a back exit. The front will be watched."

They darted to the back of the building, leaping over bars, heaps of metal, wood, and anything else in the way.

"Here! A door!" the detective gasped as he reached the wall. He yanked the handle, but the door was locked. "Come on, Phil!" he directed, taking a few paces back. "Three, two, one, go!"

They rushed at the door, plowing their shoulders into it at the same time.

"And again!"

They stepped back and charged once more. This time, the door burst open and they found themselves in a small room like an office. The window was broken, and the detective didn't waste a moment.

"Follow me!" he directed as he led the way, clambering up on the desk. He knelt upon it, leaning through the opening and slipping one foot on the window frame. In a moment, he was gone.

Phil repeated the motions with the detective watching from outside. He crouched on the window frame and leaped to the ground, but his one arm did not follow. He landed in the grass, staggered, and lost balance with his left arm still stuck inside the window.

"What's happened?"

"My watch! It's caught on something!" Phil struggled furiously, reaching inside to free himself. "There's a hook on the wall just here. My watch strap is caught!"

The detective bounded forward, reaching up. "Don't pull! There!"

He had managed to unclasp the strap, freeing Phil's wrist from the snagged watch. "Now run," he said, "as though your life depended on it."

****

"Five!"

Andy looked around, frantically searching for an idea. *If I was armed, I could hold them both up at gunpoint. If I was closer, I could sneak up and punch that big guy. If . . .*

"Four!"

Andy suddenly caught sight of a medium-sized, smooth rock on the ground nearby. He picked it up.

"Three!"

He turned the rock over, mentally judging its weight. *I think I could just manage . . .*

"Two!"

Shooting up a quick prayer, Andy jumped to his feet, swung his arm back, and hurled the rock as hard as he could at the large man. To the boy's surprise, it hit the man full force on the side of the head, causing the remote to fall from his hands. Apparently dazed, the man doubled over and slumped against the car. Mr. Larone showed his surprise at the turn of events by letting out a squeal, and then hollering, "Don't move!"

But Andy was already crouched down behind the hedge, his fingers clasping another rock.

"Get that remote!" Mr. Larone commanded. "Vince! I said get that remote! Never mind, I'll get it. You get that boy!"

Andy's heart skipped a beat as he heard the last instruction. He knew he couldn't run away and leave Phil to his fate. He gripped the rock until his knuckles turned white and squeezed himself against the hedge. Seconds ticked by, with no sound from either of the men. The next moment, Vince lunged around the hedge with surprising speed. Andy reflexively threw the rock, but it glanced off Vince's shoulder, and as Andy turned to flee, the man caught him around the waist. Andy fought hard, kicking out and flailing his arms, but Vince just swung the boy horizontally under one arm, grabbed his wrists in the other hand, and marched back to the car.

"Let me go!" Andy cried out. "Let me go! Let me go!" As they rounded the hedge, he saw Mr. Larone with the remote. "Don't! Don't do it! This is murder! There are people inside! This is murder! Stop!"

"Keep quiet!" Vince roared. "Or else!"

What happened next was too sudden for Andy to remember clearly. An arm shot out from somewhere, sending Mr. Larone sprawling, and at the same time Vince's body jerked as Andy heard a solid thump. He swayed and then collapsed on top of Andy. The weight was tremendous, and the boy found himself trapped under it in darkness, being pressed to the ground. Then the weight lifted somewhat and light appeared again.

"Help! Help!" Andy screamed.

"It's okay," a familiar voice said.

"Are you all right?" another asked in an accent.

The rest of Vince's weight lifted and a face peered down at Andy in concern. Andy jumped to his feet, wobbled unsteadily, and then collapsed to his knees, the trauma of the last hour clearly taking its toll on his body.

"Are you hurt?"

Someone crouched down beside him, and Andy threw his arms around the figure's shoulders.

"Phil! Phil!" came Andy's voice, muffled through sobs.

"I'm here. It's okay."

"I thought you were going to . . ." Andy's voice trailed off before he could finish.

Phil just nodded, patting the boy's shoulder sympathetically.

While the brothers regained composure, Detective Mortimer retrieved the remote and carefully took the batteries out. He took a few steps and then bent over to pick something up. He put it to his ear. "Hello? Good—hello, Dispatcher. This is Detective Mortimer Jones requesting immediate police assistance . . ."

Andy quickly pulled his sleeve across his face, but his cheeks still glistened in the moonlight. "Wh-what happened?" he asked, his voice wavering.

Phil briefly recounted the events of the last few minutes, which had felt more like hours, and finished by saying, "Then we doubled back around the warehouse and managed to sneak up behind those crooks and knock them out."

Andy nodded. "So—so that's why Mr.—Larone fell over and Vince almost crushed me."

"Yes."

"The police are on their way," Detective Mortimer announced, striding over to hand Phil his phone. "You called them, Andy?"

"Yes, sir. I couldn't—say anything though."

"It was good thinking. The dispatcher heard the commotion and decided to listen in. He's sending men over. To be honest, I can't wait to examine that warehouse and find out what these men were trying to hide."

CHAPTER 21

The police arrived a few minutes later and arrested the still-drowsy Mr. Larone and Vince. The others congratulated the detective, Phil, and Andy when they heard the full story.

"That was a very dangerous situation tonight," one officer said. "Obviously, you are three brave men," he finished with a grin in Andy's direction.

"Yes. You fellas must have proud parents," another added.

"That's right," Phil said, resting his hand on Andy's shoulder. "I almost didn't bring my 'little' brother along tonight—and boy, would I have regretted that!"

"So would I," Detective Mortimer agreed.

Andy pulled his cheeks into a dutiful smile, but looked down at his shoes. There was something still nagging him, something that made him feel unworthy of the praise. He was grateful that nobody seemed to notice.

"When can the warehouse be searched?" Phil asked. "My father and Mr. Wilbur could be in there."

"We first have to get our specialist bomb-disposal team to give us the go-ahead," the first officer answered. "You boys are free to leave. You must be exhausted."

"Can we stay around?" Phil asked.

"I think you'd better go," Detective Mortimer said. "Your mother won't stop worrying until she knows you're safe and sound under the same roof again. I'll let you know as soon as I can what we find."

Phil hesitated, and then slowly agreed. "All right. Thank you, Detective."

"No. Thank you, boys. For everything," Detective Mortimer replied.

The brothers turned to walk the rest of the way to the car.

"What a night," Phil breathed.

Andy stifled a yawn. "I'm exhausted, but there's no way I'll sleep a wink when I get home."

"Me neither."

They climbed into the car, and Phil started the engine. "Hey, Andy?"

"Yes?"

"I want to say a proper 'thank you' for all that you did tonight. If it wasn't for you, well . . . things would have ended very differently. You saved my life, you really did, and I want you to know how proud I am to have you as my brother."

"Oh, uh, sure. Thank you for—well, firstly for surviving." Andy managed a grin while Phil chuckled. "Secondly, for saving me from Vince, and thirdly . . ."

"For bringing you along?" Phil suggested.

"Yes."

"You're more than welcome." Phil smiled. "The way things turned out tonight, you can come *anytime*. But honestly, thank you for being 'strong and of good courage.' It's hard to respect a coward. I'm very glad you're not one."

Andy gulped. "You're welcome."

The brothers arrived home and were met at the door by their mother, whose nerves seemed strained to their breaking point.

"Thank the Lord you're back! Are you boys all right? What happened? Why were you away so long? Did you manage to follow Mr. La—Phil! What happened to your head?"

The brothers had come into the kitchen, where the bright light cast a glow on a lump forming just above Phil's eyebrow.

"My head?" Phil repeated, feeling it gingerly. "I don't know. I'm sure it's nothing to worry about."

"It's not *nothing*, Philip Baker! You're going to have a black, blue, and brown bruise for weeks! Now please tell me what happened while I get some ice."

Andy collapsed into a chair while Phil commenced recounting the night's events. Andy felt physically, mentally, and emotionally drained, with a deep discouragement in his heart that he could not shake.

Once Mrs. Baker had looked over Phil's bruise and provided an ice-pack for it, she busied herself with making hot cocoa while she listened.

"Then we waited and waited for Detective Mortimer to come back and tell us whether the coast was clear or not. When he didn't return, I went in to find him, telling Andy to stay outside."

"Outside!" Mrs. Baker gasped, her spoon pausing in the air on its way to the sugar jar. "You left Andy outside the warehouse, by himself, while you went in to find Detective Mortimer?"

"Well, yes, but I gave him my phone and told him to call the police if I wasn't back in five minutes. There wasn't anything else I could have done. Taking him inside could have been more dangerous."

"And that turned out to be the case," Andy added.

"I see." Mrs. Baker nodded slowly. "Go on."

Phil continued with the story, and then said, "When I got back outside, Andy was very shaken up and told me some startling news. Tell your side of the story."

"Well, I was sitting outside when I heard footsteps. Mr. Larone and his accomplice ran past me to their car and drove away, mentioning something about a detonator as they passed."

"Detonator!" Mrs. Baker's eyes grew wide as she glanced from one son to the other.

"That was my reaction too," Phil said. "I raced back into the warehouse to warn the detective, telling Andy to get away from the building fast." He related the rest of the details as Mrs. Baker set down two mugs of sweet and steaming cocoa. Then he said, "Andy, please tell us what happened to you."

"Which part?"

"From the time I left you to the time the detective and I saved you."

"Well," Andy began hesitantly, "I ran away from the warehouse, as you told me, and then fell over beside a hedge. Basically, that's when I realized Mr. Larone and Vince were in their car nearby. They were. . . uh—" he paused, considering how to use as few words as possible, "—uh . . . hoping to blow up the warehouse, and then a little later Vince came around the hedge and caught me. That's when Phil and Detective Mortimer appeared. Your turn, Phil."

Phil frowned. "It sounds like no big deal when you put it that way. You told the police a lot more than that! Mother, Andy saved my life—and the detective's life—by refusing to be a coward—"

Andy squirmed in his seat, and let out an inward sigh of relief when the phone rang. "I'll get it!" he exclaimed eagerly as he leaped forward and grabbed the receiver.

"Hello, this is the Baker residence; Andrew speaking. Detective! Yes, sir. She's right here. Yes. Goodbye." He held out the receiver to his mother, whispering, "Detective Mortimer wants to speak to you."

"Hello, Detective Mortimer? Yes, thank the Lord they're both safe and sound." Mrs. Baker glanced at her two boys. "They were just telling me what happened. Yes?" She paused. "I'm sorry; what did you just say?"

The boys looked up sharply at her change of tone. Her eyebrows were high and her lips were parted in an expression of shock.

"Hospital! Really? Yes, yes, I understand. Can we all . . . yes?" She paused again. "Hannah can't see him now? All right. We'll head over now. Thank you for the call, Detective. Goodbye."

She set down the phone and blinked rapidly. "Your father and Mr. Wilbur have been found!"

CHAPTER 22

Mrs. Baker and the boys soon found themselves plodding down hospital corridors to find the ward they had been directed to. After the detective's phone call, Mrs. Baker had awakened Mrs. Wilbur and explained the situation, whereupon the three awake Bakers had left to head straight for the hospital.

Detective Mortimer had said there was no point in Mrs. Wilbur coming along, as she'd just have to wait a long time to see her husband.

How much farther? Andy felt like asking. He was weary, but full of an irritable, unsettled tension after all the stressful events of the night. Looking up, he decided Phil felt the same way.

They soon turned down another corridor, and then entered a waiting area, empty except for a few seats nearby. As soon as the Bakers appeared, one of the seated figures arose.

"Charlie!" Mrs. Baker exclaimed, rushing forward and throwing her arms around her husband. "Thank the Lord! I was so worried about you."

"Father!" Phil and Andy chorused.

Mr. Baker looked rather haggard, with cloudy eyes, a color-drained face, and wrinkles that were more prominent than usual. But he gave a relieved smile as he hugged his wife back and gave her a kiss, and then turned to the boys and laid a hand on each of their shoulders.

"I heard what you did tonight, boys, and I want to let you know how grateful I am to both of you."

"You're welcome," Phil replied. "The Lord looked after us all."

"Yes. I'm glad you're safe, Father," Andy said.

"I can't wait to hear what happened," Mrs. Baker put in. "From the little that the detective told me, you were in a lot of danger."

"It's true," Mr. Baker said, "but I'd really appreciate getting home and comfortable before I plunge into the story again."

"Of course, of course!" Mrs. Baker agreed quickly.

Mr. Baker turned to the men who had been seated beside him. One of them was Detective Mortimer. He stepped forward.

"Here, Phil," he said, holding out the other's gold watch. "I thought you might want this back."

"Thank you!" Phil said gratefully. "I was worried I'd never see it again."

Mr. Baker reached out to shake the detective's hand. "Thanks so much for helping us once again."

"My pleasure. Do let me know if you need anything." Then, "Goodbye," he said to them all, "and see if you can catch some sleep. We all look like we need it!"

The Bakers stopped at the nursing station to ask after Mr. Wilbur, and were told that he was comfortable, but couldn't have any visitors.

"Call a bit later in the morning," the nurse suggested.

Phil could not believe the time was just after six a.m. when they arrived home from the hospital. Though they all tried to be quiet, a few seconds after they walked in there was a pattering sound on the stairs. Abby rushed into the kitchen, already dressed, and took in the scene with an expression of delight.

"Father! You're home!" she cried as she ran forward.

"Yes, it's true," he chuckled faintly, patting her back as she hugged him.

"When I woke up, Mrs. Wilbur told me you had been found," she explained, "but I still don't know how. Are you hurt?"

"No, not much."

Abby then glanced from one face to another, especially at her brothers. "Why do you boys look so old and tired? Phil! What happened to your head?"

"It's a long story, dear," Mrs. Baker replied.

Mrs. Wilbur came downstairs at that point, looking as though she'd hardly slept. "How is Jed?" she asked.

They repeated what the nurse had told them, and then Mr. Baker added, "His arm was treated as soon as we arrived at the hospital. You'll be able to visit him soon."

"What can I get you to drink?" Mrs. Baker asked her husband. "The kettle's finished boiling."

"I'd love a cup of coffee."

"Would you like something to eat?" Abby suggested, starting to feel hungry herself.

"Yes, please. Scrambled eggs on toast is just what I feel like."

Abby had half turned to go when she looked back at her brothers with a grin and said, "I'm sure you two don't feel like anything, right?"

"Not at all," Andy said dryly with a shake of his head, "but since you're already making toast . . ."

"We'll just make sure you get enough practice," Phil finished.

They were each soon supplied with a steaming drink and a mound of scrambled eggs on toast with a quick accompaniment of fried mushrooms and tomatoes. They sat comfortably in the living room, and Tom, who had just joined them, was snuggled close to Mr. Baker.

"It was at the point that we found out about the explosives that Jed and I began frantically trying to free ourselves," Mr. Baker said, finally reaching the critical point of his story. "We knew that if somebody came to rescue us, the result could be tragic. After a long and painful time, I managed to free the bonds around my feet. Then I continued kicking against the one end of the crate, to loosen it. I had stopped for a rest when I heard voices. Both Jed and I started hollering warnings as loud as we could in our weakened state, and it was with great angst that we could almost feel time ticking. But nothing happened, and the voices died away.

"Some hours later, we heard more of them, so we started yelling again. There was a crash, as of a door being broken down, and then I heard my crate being opened. When the lid was finally pried off, I found myself surrounded by police officers, and there, standing humbly behind them, was Detective Mortimer. The police set to work opening Jed's crate, and then rushed us both to the hospital while I filled them in on our story."

"You must have been starving and extremely thirsty!" Mrs. Baker gasped. "Would you like more coffee? Or water? Or toast?"

"No, thank you, dear." Mr. Baker shook his head. "We were looked after at the hospital."

"So you were in the warehouse all along?" Phil asked. "I didn't hear shouts when the detective and I were trying to get away."

"We were in a little room—a side office."

Phil's eyebrows rose. "That must have been like the one we escaped through."

"Yes," his father said. "The detective said it was."

"How was Jed when he was rescued?" Mrs. Wilbur asked, one hand covering her mouth in concern.

Mr. Baker chose his words carefully. "He didn't look too well when I first saw him, but his arm has been treated since then. I'm sure he's resting." At that moment, he stifled an involuntary yawn.

"You should probably *all* be resting," Mrs. Baker suggested, glancing over at Phil and Andy, whose eyelids were drooping.

"I don't think I'll be able to sleep, but a rest sounds good," Phil muttered. Andy nodded.

"Aren't you tired too, Alice?" Mrs. Wilbur asked. "I'm sure you haven't slept since the boys left."

"Well, no," Mrs. Baker admitted. "I would appreciate a short rest."

"You do that. I'm going to take my kids to the hospital as soon as possible," Mrs. Wilbur replied.

"And Tom and I can take care of the chores," Abby volunteered.

"Abby, would you mind feeding—" Andy began, but Abby held up her hand with a smile.

"Of course I don't mind. Tom and I can tackle the most important chores together—right, Tom? Andy, you go and rest now, because I want to hear what you did on your night adventure as soon as you wake up."

In his exhaustion, Andy let out what was meant to be an inward groan. Abby laughed, thinking he was being sarcastic. Little did she imagine that he was not.

While Abby and Tom went outside, the others headed upstairs for some badly-needed rest. Andy trudged into his room and set down his flashlight, and was about to fall on his bed when he noticed his pillow was gone.

He moaned and shuffled to retrieve it and his bed-covers from Phil's room, where he and the other boys had camped the previous night. Seth and John were stirring when he went inside.

"Is it my turn to keep watch yet?" John muttered as he raised himself on one elbow and rubbed his eyes.

"No," Andy answered moodily, grabbing his pillow.

"It's light already! Why isn't Seth awake?" John slipped out of bed to sit dutifully at the laptop. "He didn't sleep through his turn, did he?"

"Yes, actually, he did."

"He did?" John asked, his eyes widening.

"Andy, don't be so grumpy!" came the voice from Phil's bed. "It's nothing to worry about, John, and no, you don't have to keep watch anymore. The crooks have already been caught."

"They have?" John gasped.

"Wh-what are you fellas talking about?" Seth mumbled in a groggy voice. "Isn't it a bit early to be arguing?"

"We're not arguing," John replied. "Seth, the crooks have already been caught!"

"What crooks? Oh, you mean Mr. Larone?" Seth asked, suddenly sitting up. "How did that happen?"

"It's a long story." Andy moaned. "Ask Phil."

"You mean you were there when it happened? No way! What did you do?" Seth pressed.

"Nothing much."

"Were you in danger?" John asked.

"Andy just saved our lives," Phil said. "That's all. Nothing much, right?" he added dryly.

"You were all going to die? Wow! And you're a hero, Andy? How awesome!" Seth continued.

"How did you save everybody?" John asked.

"I'll tell you later," Andy mumbled.

"That's awesome!" Seth cried. "I want to hear all about it!"

"Just—let—me—sleep!" Andy exclaimed in exasperation.

As Andy dragged his bed-covers into his room and shut the door behind him, he heard Seth say, "Wish I could have been there . . ."

Andy dumped the pillow and covers on his bed and collapsed in a heap, closing his tired eyes. *All these questions! I wish they would stop! How can I possibly explain that I'm not a hero at all?*

The fast-paced events of the past few hours replayed themselves across his mind in vivid detail. He shut his eyes tighter. The scene by the hedge flashed before him, and he watched as the second rock glanced off Vince's shoulder. He replayed those few seconds over and over, trying to imagine what would've happened if he'd only thrown the rock straight. Finally, he managed to correct the scene. The rock knocked Vince unconscious, and he boldly ran around the hedge, somehow taller and stronger than before, to challenge Mr. Larone. The man was immediately intimidated and handed over the remote. Andy bound the two villains just as Phil appeared, admiration in his eyes as he beheld the victory of his heroic brother . . .

Heroic was the last thing on Andy's mind as he slid into a deep, deep sleep.

CHAPTER 23

The Wilburs returned to the Bakers' house late that afternoon after spending hours with Mr. Wilbur. Emily rushed down to the stables, finding Abby in the tack room.

"Abby! Oh, there you are!"

"Hi, Emily. How's your father?"

"He's fine, thanks. He'll stay in hospital just until the doctor says it's safe for him to leave."

"That's best. Did you hear the news?"

"What news?"

"The news of what the crooks were up to," Abby answered.

"No! Tell me all about it."

"The police found the three crates from your property in a shed that was a safe distance away from the warehouse."

"What was inside them?"

"Listen to this—they were *all* full of those ancient artifacts!"

"Wow! Amazing!"

"The crooks wanted to blow a big hole under the warehouse in order to

211

hide those crates!" Abby said.

"So that's what the explosives were for!" Emily cried.

"Yes, but that's only half of the news," Abby continued. "They also found an extremely old letter hidden in the last one!"

"They did?" Emily gasped. "Who was it from?"

"That's the part I want you to guess."

Emily's brow wrinkled. "Hmm . . . was it written by Mr. Larone when he was a young boy?"

Abby laughed. "Mr. Larone isn't *extremely old!*"

"No, I guess not." Emily giggled. "That guess made no sense. Let me try again. Umm . . . Mr. Larone's grandfather?"

"No, he's not ancient enough either. This letter was from—you won't believe this—Haggai Larone!"

"Haggai Larone?" Emily repeated. "You mean the man who fought with Victor over the ring?"

"The very same."

"No way! That's incredibly awesome! What did it say?"

Abby pulled a sheet of note paper from her pocket. "I jotted down all I could remember from when I heard it read. It basically goes like this:

'To my dear son Barnaby,

'Do not be surprised when you hear the news that I am killed. My dying at the hands of Red Dirk and his outlaws has been bound to happen for a long while.

'I will not waste my time nor yours with fancy words, but will get right down to business. You can have the silver stirrups I filched from old Jackson and that gold ring I took from Victor James. Under the bed is thirty dollars. Give half to your mother.

'Do not, under any circumstances, tell Victor anything about that ring. I know he will come after it. This is a matter of family honor.

'Time is short. I must go. Give my best to the family.

'Your loving Pa,

'Haggai.'"

Emily let out a long breath as Abby finished. "We finally have proof that the Jameses have a claim over the Larones! That's great news."

"It certainly is," Abby agreed. "I am very grateful the letter was discovered."

"Does that mean that Haggai hid those artifacts?"

Abby shook her head. "It can't mean that. Probably the letter was preserved as a family heirloom and passed down a few generations before one of the Larones hid it in the crates."

"Well, now that those artifacts have been recovered, does this mean we're, like, millionaires?"

"I don't know," Abby said. "Phil has been trying to research the different laws regarding such finds, but even he's not sure yet."

Emily frowned. "Those crates were found on our property, and—it's not really fair if we don't get to keep them. Can't we?"

"It's not that straightforward," Abby said. "Those artifacts might be the spoils of grave-robbers, you know, people who stole treasures from graves. If those crates contained old coins or money instead, then they would probably be yours, but since they're not, they don't fall under the laws of treasure trove."

"That's really not fair," Emily muttered with a slight pout. "Don't we deserve some kind of reward for all this trouble?"

Abby hesitated for a moment, being tempted to agree with Emily's attitude. Biting her lip, she recalled her mother's words from a few days before. She took a deep breath.

"Come on, Em," she managed. "We've got so much to be grateful for. Our fathers have been rescued, the criminals are caught, your land is safe, *and* the mystery is solved. Don't you think we've already got much more than we actually *deserve*?"

Emily's pout disappeared and her eyebrows rose a little in surprise. "Well, I, uh . . . I mean, of course I agree, just . . . well, it would be kind of nice . . ."

Her voice faltered.

"Do you want to go for a ride?" Abby asked. Her heart had filled with a joy she couldn't describe. *Victory!* she thought. *Thank you, Father!*

"Oh, sure," Emily stammered. "I'd love to."

"You can borrow Snowdrop," Abby continued. "Here's her tack."

The girls headed out on the trail to the forest, and had been chatting about all sorts of things when Emily suddenly said, "Abby, can I ask you something?"

"Of course," Abby responded.

"How is it possible that you and all your siblings are, like, so close?"

Abby blinked in surprise. Emily had broached the subject she had just been hoping to talk about!

"Do you mean you want to know how we get on with each other?"

Emily nodded.

"Well, I'll just start off by saying that we weren't always this peaceful, and we still have our disagreements at times." Abby grinned slightly. "No matter how much we know, there's always more to grow in."

Emily sighed. "You can say that again."

"I guess it boils down to the fruits of the Spirit, really. Love—you do to others as you'd have them do to you. Long-suffering—you're patient with others' irritating habits and downfalls. Self-control—you rein yourself in from exploding when others step on your toes."

"That sounds very difficult. Especially with my siblings."

"Difficult? No, it's impossible."

Emily gave her friend a flabbergasted stare. "What? Impossible—then what's the point?"

"It's impossible *except for God's grace*," Abby corrected. "'With God all things are possible.'"

****

Andy stumbled through the day, moaning about little things. Most people thought he was just over-tired, but Phil had other suspicions.

"Well, it's been an exceptionally eventful few days," Phil said, as he, his father, and Andy sat on the porch that evening. "We can be grateful that the Lord protected us all."

"You're right." Mr. Baker nodded. "He works in miraculous ways."

"And He uses us as His instruments, right?" Phil put in.

"That's true. He worked through each of you as you were willing to lay aside personal fears for the benefit of others."

Phil stood up. "Yes. I'm sorry Father, but I should leave you two now. There's some work I really ought to catch up on . . ."

"That's fine," Mr. Baker said, giving Phil a knowing look. "You go ahead with that. We can chat later."

Mr. Baker started humming a hymn as Phil walked back inside. Then he said, "You know, Andy, I don't think I heard first-hand from you what happened last night."

"No, I don't think so," Andy replied, shifting his weight. "Phil's much better at describing events than I am."

"That doesn't normally stop you," Mr. Baker said with a smile.

"No, not normally," Andy admitted.

"Something tells me you don't want to talk about what happened," Mr. Baker continued, "not even to Abby, or Tom, or Seth. Now that's pretty unusual, don't you think?"

Andy nodded. "Yes, sir."

"Is there a reason for this 'sudden and inexplicable reticence,' to use Detective Mortimer's vocabulary?" Mr. Baker asked with humor in his voice, but his expression was serious.

"Yes, sir." Andy gulped. He took a breath, and then hesitatingly began. "Father, I've always longed to be in the thick of adventures, like Phil always is."

"Naturally," Mr. Baker encouraged as Andy's voice trailed off.

"I've always wanted to be a hero, like he is. And I've never really got the chance."

"I wouldn't say that. You've done more heroic things in your life than most boys ever do. Why, I could recall a number of times you have displayed—well, great bravery."

Andy dropped his eyes. "That's the thing," he muttered miserably. "I'm not brave. I've always thought I was, and that I could be a hero, but—but now I know that I'm not."

Mr. Baker's eyes widened. "No? Why the sudden change?"

"Father, last night, for the first time, I knew deep down that I was very—" he swallowed hard, "—very afraid."

"Oh, really?" Mr. Baker's eyebrows lifted.

Andy nodded in shame, his voice dropping to a hoarse whisper. "Yes, sir. For awhile I was actually *paralyzed* with fear. I was helpless. I wanted to save Phil and Detective Mortimer so badly, but there was nothing for me to do."

"And then?"

"Well, I remembered a Scripture, and I heard the bad guys preparing to blow up the building, and then I got the simple idea of stopping them with a rock."

"And you stopped them?"

"No, only delayed them. They captured me, and it was Phil to the rescue again."

There was silence as they both thought for a moment.

"You know, Son, I don't think that was a bad thing for you to experience."

"It wasn't?" Andy asked quickly.

"Not at all. Do you recall that verse in 1 Peter that says, 'God resists the proud, but gives grace to the humble'? Just think about it this way. If we could solve our own problems and could think of some way to save the day in every situation, imagine how proud and independent we'd get. We would think we were invincible. God would have to resist us in our pride until we came to the realization that we can do nothing without Him."

Mr. Baker looked up at the darkening sky, which was illuminated by a big, round moon.

"You mentioned Phil more than once. Does he strike you as a proud person? Is he loud, disrespectful, arrogant, or unkind?"

Andy shook his head slowly. "No."

"He is humble, and therefore God gives him grace in tough situations. You said that it was only once you were paralyzed by fear and saw your own helplessness that you got an idea of how to delay the criminals. Don't you think that was the Lord teaching you a lesson? That He would resist your pride, but give you grace when you're humble?"

Andy sighed. "Yes, sir. I suppose I have been pretty boastful recently, trying to prove to the Wilburs that I'm fearless."

"Fearless?"

"Yes. It hit me hard last night, then, when I realized I was so afraid. I've gotten very frustrated by everybody telling me how brave I was, when it isn't true and I don't want to admit it."

Mr. Baker nodded. "Extreme disappointment in self can be just a manifestation of pride—particularly when you want to prove something to others and you fail. Are you saying that because you were afraid, you weren't courageous, or you weren't fearless?"

"Both."

"Don't confuse the two. They're very different. Fearlessness is the absence of fear. I would dare to say that courage is action *in spite* of fear."

"You would?" Andy frowned.

"Oh, yes. You were very scared, but you acted in spite of that fear by God's grace. For that reason, you were courageous. Not because you were fearless, but because you laid down your personal safety for others."

****

Phil walked inside the house and passed his mother humming contentedly in the living room. He was about to head upstairs to his room, striding two stairs at a time as he normally did, when he hesitated in thought. A puzzled

217

expression came over his face, and he retraced his steps to the living room.

"Mother?"

"Hmm?" Mrs. Baker responded, looking up from the hem she was adjusting on Tom's overalls.

"May I ask you something?"

"Go ahead." She paused in her stitching at his tone.

"I know it's quite a strange thing to ask," he began, his voice trailing off as he glanced down at his wrist. Then he quickly said, "Oh, don't worry. I'm sure it's nothing important."

He had turned to leave when Mrs. Baker called, "Wait a minute, Phil. You're going to have to tell me what it is you were going to ask, else I'll be wondering about it for the rest of the evening!"

"Well, it's probably nothing, but . . . I was just wondering . . ."

"Yes?"

"Last night, when Andy and I sneaked over to Mr. Larone's house, you asked—you asked if I had my watch with me," he finished in a puzzled voice. "I couldn't understand why, and wondered if there was any particular reason."

"Oh-h," Mrs. Baker breathed, as if she almost regretted encouraging the question. She seemed to be trying to figure out what to say. "Well. That's a . . . a valid question . . . but I can't give you an answer without talking to your father first."

Phil's eyebrows rose in surprise. "Really? Okay."

Much later, once Tom was asleep, the twins sat together in Abby's room. Andy had just finished telling her what had happened the previous night. It seemed easier after the discussion with Mr. Baker.

"Is that what you were grumpy about?" Abby suddenly asked with a merry laugh. "You're funny, And. Why, you saved four people last night—Phil, Father, the detective, and Mr. Wilbur. You're becoming a . . . well, a literal lifesaver! That's nothing to be ashamed of."

"I know," he said, "but my fearlessness, which I was proud of, was shattered. So hearing everyone congratulating my bravery was very frustrating.

I'm glad I know there's a difference between the two—and that pride doesn't pay."

"Ah." Abby nodded wisely. "So am I."

Her brother frowned. "What do you mean?"

"I'm also glad you've had the chance to learn this lesson. If you hadn't, I wouldn't know what to do."

"You mean you noticed my behavior in front of Seth?"

Abby smiled. "Of course I did. You're much more pleasant as plain, old Andy."

"Plain? Old?" He chuckled, and then leaned back with a sigh of contentment. "I can't believe that camera on the porch worked."

"It was a great idea."

"And the first time I threw the rock, I didn't really think it would hit Vince right on the head. Mr. Larone got such a fright! You should have heard his shriek!"

Abby giggled. "I can hardly imagine it. You and Vince sound like David and Goliath."

They lapsed into silence, Andy thinking. Then he perked up, a strange expression spreading over his face. "You know, I've just realized something."

"What?"

"Well, Phil and the detective arrived at just the right moment to rescue me."

It was Abby's turn to look thoughtful. "Uh, yes they did. That means . . . ?"

"If they'd arrived one minute later, it would be too late to save me from the bad guys. And if they'd arrived one minute earlier, I wouldn't have learned to be humble." Andy's speech slowed, amazement in each syllable. "Every single delay inside the warehouse, from Detective Mortimer being trapped, to the locked office door, to Phil's watch getting stuck, was perfectly planned. Perfectly—timed."

Abby fingered her necklace, her jaw slack as she pondered this revelation for awhile. "You're right," she breathed, tears pricking her eyes. "No sequence of events is beyond God's control. He is good, Andy. So very, very good."

Andy nodded silently. A verse sprang to his mind, and he whispered it softly. "'All things work together . . .'" He let out a breath. "That one will never get old."

Phil appeared at the door just a few moments later, saying, "Father and Mother asked me to call you. They want to tell us something."

The twins hurried down the stairs behind him, finding their parents waiting in the living room. Tom's adjusted overalls lay hanging over an armrest.

"Children," Mr. Baker began, "your mother and I have agreed that it's time to let you know about something we've kept a secret until now."

Mrs. Baker nodded.

The children settled down comfortably on the other sofa to await the rest of this mysterious address.

"You will of course remember," Mr. Baker continued, "the way the Verton jewelry gang was caught some time ago."

He paused as they nodded emphatically.

"And I'm sure you remember the occasion on which Phil, Abby, and your cousin Millie were rewarded for involvement in the case."

Again, there were vigorous nods.

"When Detective Mortimer's father told me that he wanted to make a piece of jewelry to thank you, I had an immediate request to make. Considering all the dangers you children had been exposed to, especially Abby and Phil, I thought it would be prudent to somehow be able to keep track of your locations. Jewelry seemed the perfect idea."

"Tracking devices," Phil muttered in amazement, staring at the gold watch on his wrist.

"That's right," Mr. Baker said. "I asked Mr. Jones to install a tiny tracking device in your watch, Phil, and your locket, Abby."

"Is that why we've been working on miniature communications devices and trying to get them to work off electromagnetic waves?" Phil asked excitedly.

Mr. Baker nodded. "Exactly. I have often thought that huge improvements could be made by enabling the devices to contact each other, as well as by tapping into the electromagnetic waves all around us as a power source. Your mother and I decided it would be best not to tell any of you about the devices unless absolutely necessary, but seeing as Abby only wears her locket on special occasions, it can't really do much good."

"Oh," Abby said, her cheeks flushing pink. "I didn't realize that wearing it was so important."

"Of course you didn't," Mrs. Baker said kindly. "When Phil and Andy went out to catch Mr. Larone last night, I wanted to be sure I could keep track of where they were, if necessary."

"What a genius idea," Andy thought aloud.

"Well, it has proven to give us at least a little peace of mind," Mr. Baker said with a nod. "After the devices were installed in the watch and locket, we decided to install one in your flashlight, Andy. You seem to take it with you just about everywhere."

Andy's eyes widened in surprise and delight. "There's really one in my flashlight? That's—well, as Seth would say, that's *awesome*!"

The others laughed.

"Now you know the secret," Mr. Baker continued, "but of course I must ask you to keep it quiet from everyone, even Tom. We think it's unnecessary for him to know yet. The fewer the people who know about our devices, the better. That way the devices will be much more likely to be helpful if we're in danger in the future."

CHAPTER 24

Mr. Wilbur was allowed to leave the hospital the next day, and that evening the two families and Detective Mortimer met at the Bakers' house to give thanks for the Lord's protection over all of them. They had a lovely time, especially when they gathered in the living room after supper for a relaxed chat and the chance to recount the events.

"Well, thank the Lord we're all safe!" Mrs. Baker said, glancing around the group.

"God is good," Abby said.

"All the time!" Tom added.

"You must have worried about us quite a lot over these past few days, Mother," Phil said.

"I certainly have," Mrs. Baker responded in a serious tone, but with a playful expression. "This sort of dangerous adventure has happened to us at least three times already. I hope it doesn't become a habit!"

"Thanks to that old letter, we know for sure that the ring originally belonged to Victor James and was stolen by Haggai Larone," Mr. Baker said. "Because it was inscribed with a clue to the crates, we can guess that a Larone was responsible for hiding those artifacts."

"And the James family is innocent," Mr. Wilbur added. "Boy, am I relieved!"

"I suppose that means we can give the ring straight to Mr. James, right?" Phil asked.

"The story isn't that straightforward, I'm afraid," Detective Mortimer said. "The police questioned Mr. Larone, and he admitted he was guilty of stealing the ring. He claims this is because it belongs to him and he would never have been able to prove it without giving away the secret of the artifacts."

Phil frowned. "That's wrong, isn't it?"

"In fact, it isn't," the detective replied, pausing as surprised exclamations filled the room. "There's quite a fascinating story behind all of this, which I was pleased to finally uncover.

"Mr. Larone's grandfather, who passed away many years ago, was an exceptionally skilled archeologist, and he frequently traveled around the world to work on different digs. Whenever he left to move on to another location, the archeologists staying behind would discover that their records were wrong. As time went on, one man eventually guessed that this skilled archeologist was smuggling items from the digs and tampering with the records. This caused enough confusion to allow him to get away in time.

"Museums were contacted and warned about this archeologist, but they never heard from him. He was never convicted and, as far as the law is concerned, got away with it. Nobody knew what he had done with those artifacts, as he couldn't easily sell them without getting caught.

"We now know that he carefully concealed them on his property in the early 1900s, and wrote a riddle to pass down his family line—a riddle which hinged upon the discovery of a clue. This way, the exact location of the artifacts could be found only by one of his descendants at a time when it would be safe to sell them.

"Now, the ring that had caused so much strife between the Larone and James families had long been lost, but the archeologist knew the story, and knew what an important symbol it was for both families. That is why he chose to make a beautiful, gold ring and inscribe upon it the clue that would activate the riddle.

"As the generations passed, this story was passed on too, and many Larones searched for and failed to find the ring. Though the Larones finally left the farm, they never forgot the story of its treasure. Thus, when Bud

Larone heard of the discovery of the crates, he knew immediately that if a ring had been found too, it was the one his family had been dreaming of for years.

"He wasted no time, but began organizing an operation to find the crates and get them off the property without anybody noticing. Unfortunately for him," the detective said, smiling, "that was not to be the case."

"So the ring we found is a replica that belongs to . . . Mr. Larone?" Andy asked, his expression one of dismay.

Detective Mortimer nodded. "That is true."

"How disappointing." Abby sighed. "We didn't find poor Mr. James's family heirloom after all."

"Jed," the detective continued, "you will be pleased to know that the police have also caught Vince's friend, a fellow called Len. He's a wanted cat burglar and probably the one who stole the ring from your study."

"Really?" Mr. Wilbur responded, his eyebrows high. "I'm glad to hear about that."

"A cat burglar?" Laura muttered with a frown.

"They don't steal cats," Tom explained in a knowing voice. "They climb up walls and take things out people's windows."

Ginger-haired Zachary looked thoughtful for a moment, then lisped, "What about dog burglarth?"

Tom wrinkled his nose, stumped for awhile. "I don't know. Maybe they steal things from holes in the garden."

"If the ring belongs to Mr. Larone, what about the artifacts?" Phil asked in concern.

"Those were stolen goods, so the Larone family has no claim to them. Jed has decided to send them to a museum," the detective answered.

Phil sighed in relief, and Mr. Wilbur said, "That's right. There, they can be looked after properly and appreciated by hundreds of people."

Seth frowned. "But they were on our land. Doesn't that make them ours?"

"They were still stolen to begin with," Andy pointed out.

"Okay, so we're selling them to the museum?"

"No, they're not ours to sell," Mr. Wilbur answered.

Seth's brow creased further. "I mean, that stuff must be worth thousands of dollars. Aren't we going to get a reward, or something? "

"Probably not, Son," Mr. Wilbur replied.

The adults continued talking, and did not notice Seth cup his cheek in his hand, his expression dull. The twins looked up at Phil, who had opened his mouth to say something, when Emily's voice piped up.

"You know, Seth, look around you." She motioned to the faces all around the room. "Everybody's safe and happy, and . . . we've got a great story to tell our children one day. If we focus on what we don't have, well . . . we won't see what we've been blessed with."

Phil closed his mouth, a faint smile replacing the words he had been about to say. Abby just stared at her friend in delight. *A ripple effect*, she thought. *Mother was right*!

"And besides, Seth," Andy added, "at least the artifacts are going to a museum and not Mr. Larone!"

Just then, Mr. Wilbur's phone rang. The others lowered their voices, politely trying not to overhear the conversation. They all knew when it ended because Mr. Wilbur nearly burst with enthusiasm.

"Guess what?" he cried. "That was a friend of mine from the museum! The head curator just saw my article in the paper and said that the museum has an identical ring dating back to the 1600s! It must be the original!"

"The original?" Mr. Baker repeated.

"The original! Yes, the original!" Mr. Wilbur called, nearly leaping with excitement. "It's in the museum I was planning to send the artifacts to. Maybe, once the people in charge hear the whole story, Matthew will have the chance to prove it belongs to him!"

Mr. Baker frowned. "The problem is that Matthew's evidence is anecdotal; it's all based on personal accounts. He wouldn't be able to prove anything."

"What about that drawing in his old book?" Phil pondered aloud, rubbing his chin. "It's incredibly detailed, even down to the little symbol on the inside."

"There was a drawing?" Mr. Wilbur asked quickly. "And a symbol? That would be the mark of the jeweler who made it! If the drawing and the museum ring look alike and have the same symbol, then it must—it must!—be Matthew's!"

Emily grabbed Abby's hands for a dance of delight.

"It's found!" she sang, making up the tune as she went along. "The real ring is found and Mr. James will get it, after all!"

Above all the noise and commotion, Phil tapped Andy's shoulder and said with a great, beaming smile, "If this comes about, the whole thing will have ended perfectly."

"Yes," Andy replied. "God's work is perfect—in every way."

The families gathered round in a circle, and Mr. Baker said a heartfelt prayer of acknowledgment and thanks to the Lord. Once he had concluded, Mr. Wilbur took his turn, and then the detective, and then whoever else wanted to.

In moments of silence, some of the children offered their own secret prayers. Andy found himself thinking about his brother Phil, and silently prayed, *Thank you for making Phil a model of true courage for me, Lord. Thank you for showing me that I don't have to compete with him, but can rather learn from him. Please help me to be an example like that for Tom to follow.*

Emily opened her eyes a crack and glanced at the reverent postures all around the circle. Her eyes finally came to rest on the blonde, bowed head at her shoulder. *Seth. Thank you, God, for my brother Seth. He sure can be annoying at times, and some—well, to be honest, most—of his habits irritate me a lot. But he can be helpful now and then, he lightens the mood with his good humor, and well, all in all, I'm glad you've made him my brother. Please help me always to appreciate him.*

A surge of emotion swelled in her chest as she thought about all the things she liked, no, loved about Seth, and in that moment she reached out and clasped his hand. He gave a start of surprise, but kept his eyes closed as a grin pressed his cheeks. He squeezed her hand back.

Abby's silent prayers were along different lines. *Lord, Your goodness to us is overwhelming. May You help us always to see it, and to realize that Your ways are perfect—even if we wish You had made us prettier, or taller, or more charismatic.*

I realize now that while Emily seems to be blessed with these things more than I have been, she needs Your grace and mercy just as much as any of us do. She paused as another thought struck her. *And thank you, Father, for making me a part of this family and giving me these friends. I pray that we'd always be ready to do what's right, no matter what adventures—or challenges—may await us.*

The End

SCRIPTURES USED
IN THE STORY

Proverbs 29:11, "A fool vents all his feelings, But a wise man holds them back."

Leviticus 19:15, "You shall do no injustice in judgment. You shall not be partial to the poor, nor honor the person of the mighty. In righteousness you shall judge your neighbor."

Matthew 5:9, "Blessed are the peacemakers, For they shall be called sons of God."

Proverbs 17:14, "The beginning of strife is like releasing water; Therefore stop contention before a quarrel starts."

2 Kings 5, The story of Naaman the Leper

Psalm 91:2, "I will say of the LORD, 'He is my refuge and my fortress; My God, in Him I will trust.'"

1 Peter 5:5b, "God resists the proud, But gives grace to the humble."

Matthew 19:26, "But Jesus looked at them and said to them, 'With men this is impossible, but with God all things are possible.'"

Psalm 136:1, "Oh, give thanks to the LORD, for He is good! For His mercy endures forever."

Deuteronomy 32:4, "He is the Rock, His work is perfect; For all His ways are justice, A God of truth and without injustice; Righteous and upright is He."